Delainey's fiancé? As in future husband?

Sam circled the table and bent over Delainey's chair. "It always makes me feel warm all over when you look at me like that," he said, his voice pitched so that the two men at the table would catch every word.

His lips brushed her cheekbone and moved slowly toward her mouth. Then, as if suddenly recalling the surroundings, he pulled back. "Come on, darling. Now that you're finally done with business, let's go home...and finish this in private."

WHAT WOMEN WANT!
It could happen to you...

Every woman has dreams—deep desires, all-consuming passions, or maybe just little everyday wishes! In this brand-new miniseries from Harlequin Romance® we're delighted to present a series of fresh, lively and compelling stories by some of our most popular authors—all exploring the truth about what women *really* want.

Step into each heroine's shoes as we get up close and personal with her most cherished dreams...big *and* small!

- Is she a high-flying executive...but all she wants is a baby?
- Has she met her ideal man—if only he wasn't her new boss...?
- Is she about to marry, but is secretly in love with someone else?
- Or does she simply long to be slimmer, more glamorous, with a whole new wardrobe?

Whatever she wants, each heroine finds happiness on her own terms—and unexpected romance along the way. And she's about to discover whether Mr. Right is the answer to her dreams—or if he has a few questions of his own!

This month enjoy *Part-Time Fiancé* by Leigh Michaels.

And don't miss *Rafael's Convenient Proposal* (#3795) by Rebecca Winters on sale May 2004.

PART-TIME FIANCÉ
Leigh Michaels

WHAT WOMEN WANT!
It could happen to you...

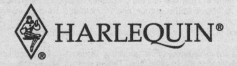

HARLEQUIN®

TORONTO • NEW YORK • LONDON
AMSTERDAM • PARIS • SYDNEY • HAMBURG
STOCKHOLM • ATHENS • TOKYO • MILAN • MADRID
PRAGUE • WARSAW • BUDAPEST • AUCKLAND

ISBN 0-373-03783-X

PART-TIME FIANCÉ

First North American Publication 2004.

This edition published by arrangement with Harlequin Books S.A.

® and TM are trademarks of the publisher. Trademarks indicated with ® are registered in the United States Patent and Trademark Office, the Canadian Trade Marks Office and in other countries.

Visit us at www.eHarlequin.com

Printed in U.S.A.

CHAPTER ONE

RUSH hour was over, but traffic was still heavy along the major streets, and it was moving slowly because of the dusting of snow which had fallen during the day. Delainey tapped her fingers on the steering wheel and held on to her patience. Normally she was unruffled by bad driving conditions, whether caused by weather or hesitant drivers or accidents stopping the normal flow of cars. In fact, she'd been stuck in so many traffic jams in her life that if she hadn't learned to keep calm she figured she'd have been dead of a heart attack long since.

But tonight was different. Tonight she was on her way home.

Finally she was able to make her turn off the boulevard and between the massive brick gateposts of the White Oaks complex. The main drive stretched out before her, twisting through a strand of mature oak trees, their branches bare now in the chill of late autumn. From the far end of the drive peeked the facade of a rambling old redbrick mansion, once a private home but now the clubhouse for the whole of White Oaks. Here and there, smaller lanes branched off the main drive, each winding through the hilly estate and ending at a cluster of modern town houses.

The third drive to the left, Delainey reminded herself. The first time she'd come here, she'd gotten thoroughly lost because all the little lanes seemed to look alike. And though there were signposts at each intersection, they were small and discreetly lettered.

Unobtrusive—and very effective at putting across the message that if you didn't know where you were going, you didn't belong at White Oaks. *Strangers and salesmen beware.*

She was surprised to see the moving van still parked in front of her town house. The engine was running, the back doors were open, and a ramp was still in place—but as far as she could see the van was empty. The movers' work must be done by now. Still, it would be nice to be able to take a look around the town house before the men left, in case she wanted something heavy shifted to a different location.

Not that she had anything terribly heavy, really. To tell the truth, Delainey was surprised the movers had used a full-size moving van when practically everything she owned would have fit on a pickup truck.

She parked behind the van and sat for a moment staring at the complex. Each of the separate buildings on the estate contained four individual town houses. The buildings were surrounded by woods, widely scattered, and set at angles so they were all but invisible to each other. Within each building, every unit faced a different direction. The effect was that each town house felt set apart, as if it were entirely alone on the grand estate.

From where Delainey sat, she could see just the front of her own town house and the side of the one next door. The two others in the building might as well not have existed at all.

The careful planning and construction was a great deal of the reason why White Oaks had been such a success ever since a development company had bought a huge, deserted and obsolete old mansion in the middle of nowhere and turned the estate into a community. It also didn't hurt, Delainey admitted, that the city had grown unexpectedly fast in that direction, and now the square mile occupied by White Oaks was smack in the middle of the action, while remaining set apart and parklike because of its sheer size. It was exclusive, private, protected, and close to work—

exactly the sort of place that up-and-coming people liked to live. People like Delainey.

The mere thought made her stomach give a strange little quiver. She wasn't used to thinking of herself in those terms—as the sort of person who moved in exclusive circles and who lived in an exclusive community. It was going to take some getting used to.

But as her new boss had pointed out, in her recently acquired position she could hardly still live in a rundown old apartment building on the edge of the industrial district. It didn't look good, he'd said. It didn't look successful—and projecting the image of success was important.

It was more than just image that had prompted her to buy the town house, of course. She had worked long and hard to earn the chance to have a home of her own. Still, it was going to take some adjustment before it all seemed real. Before it seemed that she deserved it.

She noted that the lights were blazing in her own unit—the previous occupants had left only minimal window coverings—and, in a more subdued fashion, in the town house next door. The real estate agent had told her the neighbors were a nice couple. An attorney and a software engineer, if she remembered correctly what Patty had told her. Not that Delainey was likely to have time to form friendships, so she hadn't paid a lot of attention.

Delainey opened the back door of her car to survey the few things she'd brought with her—a couple of boxes of items that were too precious to trust to the movers, a bundle of firewood that she'd bought on impulse on her lunch hour, and her briefcase. What to carry in first?

She saw movement from the corner of her eye and turned swiftly to confront the man who approached. *You've got to stop jumping like that,* she told herself. *You're not living in the inner city anymore. This is White Oaks.*

"You must be the new owner," the man said.

His voice was soft and deep and rich, with a texture

which caressed Delainey's ears in exactly the same way her cashmere scarf caressed her throat. She would have expected that the rest of him would match—an alpaca overcoat perhaps, pin-striped suit, silk tie, polished wing tips. Instead, he was wearing faded jeans that looked as if they'd shrunk to the precise shape of his body, running shoes, and a leather jacket that had definitely seen better days. His head was bare, and the crisp breeze ruffled his black hair, just a little too long over the ears. He did not look like White Oaks' usual clientele.

But that was a foolish reaction. Delainey had learned the lesson long ago—in the first week she'd worked as a teenage teller-trainee at the bank—that the customers who always looked like a million bucks were seldom the same ones who actually kept that much in their accounts.

She nodded. "Yes, I'm Delainey Hodges. And you're—?"

He didn't seem to see the hand she'd stretched out. "Any idea when your movers will be finished?"

"I'm sure they're anxious to get home," Delainey said levelly. "Why are you concerned, Mr.—?"

"Wagner. Because they've managed to block my drive, that's why."

He was right, Delainey saw. Each unit had its own garage, nestled into the town house it served but set at an angle from the entrance so it would be a less prominent part of the facade. Though the moving van was parked in front of her unit, the front wheels indeed had encroached on the neighboring drive in order to line up the ramp with Delainey's sidewalk.

"I'm sorry," she said. "The movers probably didn't realize which garage was which and thought they were blocking mine."

"No doubt. But that doesn't move the truck."

Isn't this going to be fun. This mannerless cretin lived

right next door—and if he was as touchy about other things as he was about his driveway....

An attorney and a computer engineer. She wondered which one he was. Well, Delainey told herself, the real estate person might not have been *entirely* wrong about the neighbors being a nice couple. She'd wait to see what Mr. Grumpy's wife was like—though she had to admit she was already questioning the woman's judgment. If her taste in men was any indication...

What were you just thinking about the dangers of jumping to conclusions based on first impressions? she reminded herself.

"Of course," she pointed out, "instead of merely stewing about it and lying in wait for me to arrive, you could have just asked them to move the truck."

He looked startled. "That's what I was coming over to do when I saw you drive in."

"I'll take care of it." She turned back to the car. She'd leave the boxes for now, she decided, but she could carry both the firewood and the case that held her notebook computer. She picked them up, leaned a hip against the door to shut it, and realized that the cretin-next-door hadn't moved. "Is there anything else you'd like me to do for you?" she asked pointedly. "Or are you planning to just stand out here and freeze until they move the truck?"

"On second thought," he said, "I'll go ask them myself. I must admit to being curious. I assumed from the little they took out of the van that they'd be gone within an hour. What have they been doing in there all afternoon—having a party?"

He'd actually watched while the movers unloaded her possessions? "It must be nice to have the kind of time on your hands to sit and watch the neighbors' furniture," Delainey muttered.

His eyebrows rose, as if he was wondering why she

sounded irritated. "That's my point. It didn't take all that long."

Maybe he hadn't actually been prying, Delainey told herself. She supposed there could have been other reasons why he'd been sitting by the window watching every box come off the moving van. She just couldn't happen to think of any at the moment.

"I do hope you kept a running inventory," she said sweetly. "It'll come in handy in case the movers have lost any of my possessions." She started up the sidewalk.

Just as she stepped onto the tiny porch, the front door of the town house opened and two burly men came out, one carrying an armload of neatly folded furniture pads, the other pulling a two-wheeled cart. "Just finished, Ms. Hodges," the one with the cart said. "It's all yours." He hesitated on the top step. "You're absolutely sure you want that futon downstairs?"

"Those were the instructions I left, yes."

He shrugged. "You're the boss. It just seemed odd to me, to have two big bedrooms and not a stick of furniture in either of them, only clothes and boxes—so I thought I'd better check."

"Your first house?" the cretin-next-door asked casually.

"Yes, as a matter of fact. I'm sure you're anxious to be going, Mr. Wagner, now that the truck will soon be out of your driveway." She didn't wait for an answer before going inside.

She closed the front door behind her and leaned against it, looking across the open plan of the first floor, through the entry and living area, past the stairway set off to one side and the kitchen half tucked underneath, to the glass atrium door at the back leading onto a patio.

She had seen the town house only once before, when she'd looked at it before making an offer to buy. She hadn't expected it to appear quite so different now.

But of course on that first visit it had been daylight, and

the previous occupant's furniture had still been in place. There had been posters on the walls and knickknacks on the mantel.

Now, even though the movers had left all the lights on, the rooms seemed dim and almost dingy. On the beige walls were patches of darker color where frames had hung, protecting the paint from fading. With only her own few bits of furniture in the living room—the futon, a small rocking chair, the stereo system and a television on a cart—the whole town house seemed to echo. She could hear her heartbeat, though perhaps that wasn't the silence so much as the sudden realization of the responsibility she had taken on in buying a house.

Her cell phone rang, startlingly loud in the quiet room. She glanced automatically at her watch before answering.

The voice on the other end was that of the real estate agent who had closed the deal. "How's the move going?"

"Hi, Patty. It's all finished, except for the unpacking."

"Oh, the fun part."

"Is that an offer to help?"

Patty chuckled. "Sure. I've got a free spot in my calendar a year from next April, if that's good for you."

"Thanks anyway." Delainey moved across the living room to where the black-upholstered futon sat in front of the fireplace. The movers had even plumped the cushions, and it looked almost inviting. "Patty, remember when we looked at this place and we talked about how oddly the furniture was arranged?"

"Yeah, the couch was sitting at a really strange angle."

"We should have moved it to look underneath." Delainey shifted the phone from one hand to the other and tipped her head to get a better view of the carpet. Smack in the center of the room was a black patch the size of her outstretched hand. "It looks like someone spilled India ink on the carpet, and they just set the couch on top to hide it."

"Ink? If that's actually what it is, it won't come out. I'll talk to the people at the loan company."

"You think they might actually replace the carpet?"

"I'll suggest that it would be good for customer relations—but don't get your hopes up too high."

"I won't," Delainey said. "I worked in the mortgage department at the bank for a while—long enough to know there's a whole different set of rules when it comes to houses that have been forced up for sale by the threat of repossession. *Buyer beware* is the operative phrase in situations like that."

"And you did buy the place at a pretty deep discount because everybody admits there's some work to be done."

Some work to be done? At the moment, Delainey thought, it seemed a classic understatement. "Well, right now I'd say the loan company did very well for itself. I didn't realize it would look so…abandoned."

"Every house does on moving day. Hey, if you end up stuck with the stain, you could just pretend it's a Rorschach test. It would make a great party game, having everyone interpret it."

"Thanks," Delainey said dryly. "You're a real pal, Patty."

She eyed the boxes the movers had stacked in the kitchen and decided that unpacking the toaster and her few mismatched dishes could wait awhile. The moving van was gone and there was no sign of the cretin-next-door, so she carried in her two boxes of special treasures from the car.

When she set the first one on the kitchen counter, she was startled to notice that right next to the stove, where a big ceramic fruit bowl had been strategically placed on the day she had looked at the town house, was a perfectly round scorch mark where someone had once set a sizzling skillet or a boiling kettle.

A carpet *and* a countertop needing replaced. "I wonder

what other nice little surprises I'm apt to find,'' she muttered as she began to unpack the box.

She didn't know why the previous owners had been unable to make their house payments, but she was sympathetic to their plight—and she couldn't exactly blame them for covering up the flaws. They were not only losing their home, but they'd already sacrificed the down payment they'd made when they first took out the loan. And since the loan company which carried the mortgage was looking for a quick sale which would turn just enough cash to pay the outstanding balance, the owners weren't likely to get anything from the sale at all. Only if someone offered to pay more than it took to settle the mortgage would the owners end up with a cent—so of course they'd make it look as good as they could and hope that the buyer wouldn't notice until it was too late.

Which was exactly what had happened. It hadn't occurred to Delainey to move the couch, or pick up the fruit bowl to look underneath. For that matter, she couldn't remember whether she'd actually turned on all the faucets and light switches. She'd been in a bit of a hurry that day, as she recalled.

But despite the damage, Patty was right that she had gotten a bargain. It wasn't as if she'd have to put down new carpet or tear out the kitchen countertops right away. She could live with them as they were for a while—and that was lucky, she mused. Good deal though the town house had been, it was a big leap in monthly expense from the rent she'd been paying in her shared apartment, and what the down payment had done to her savings account hadn't been pretty.

She unwrapped her grandmother's small blue china bell and set it safely on a shelf. The next bundle of tissue paper contained the silver sugar tongs she'd bought at an antique store on her last trip home. Her mother had thought the gadget a waste of money—what on earth was wrong with using a spoon?—but though Delainey couldn't have explained it, she had known she'd regret it if she walked out of the store without the tongs.

And now, finally, she might actually have a chance to use them. In the town house she could do an entirely different kind of entertaining than she'd ever tackled before. When she'd been sharing the apartment, having a few friends in for pizza and a rented movie had been a big party. Now, particularly with her new job, she would be hosting dinners and cocktail parties for clients as well. Of course, she'd need a table first, and some chairs....

Uncertain where she wanted to store the tongs, she left them lying beside the box while she unwrapped the crystal clock she'd been given for a high school graduation gift. It looked small but important in the center of the mantel, and putting it in place made her feel as if she was starting to claim the town house for her own.

She looked thoughtfully into the bare, black cavity of the fireplace. She'd never had one before. Not a real one. The fireplace in the house she'd lived in as a child had been only for show—its warm glow was provided by an orange lightbulb. And none of the apartments she'd lived in had ever been the sort to include such amenities.

The work of settling in could wait, she decided. It was her first night in her own home, and she was going to sit by her own fireside and relax. Maybe even go to sleep with the crackling of a fire to soothe her.

Upstairs, in the front bedroom where the movers had hung her clothes, she changed from her khaki-colored business suit into ivory satin pajamas and brushed out her hair until it gleamed golden brown in the bathroom mirror. She dug sheets, pillows, and blankets out of a box in the back bedroom and made up the futon, pulling it around till it sat directly in front of the fireplace. Then she found the bundle of firewood where she'd set it down right inside the front door and carried it into the living room.

The bundle was tightly wrapped in plastic, and the carrying strap had been stapled into the wood itself. She broke a fingernail, went to the kitchen to open a box to look for a knife, and cracked the tip off the knife blade before she finally managed to pry the staples loose.

"Tools," she muttered. "I'm going to have to buy some tools."

She knelt down to stack the wood in the fireplace, crisscrossing the splintery chunks as she'd seen others do. It was difficult to keep the wood from shifting and rolling, and even when she'd put it all in, it didn't seem like much of a fire. It was only a small pile. She took a deep breath and struck a match.

The wood caught fire instantly, and moments later a cloud of smoke billowed out of the fireplace and engulfed her. Coughing and choking, Delainey staggered to the atrium door at the back of the living room, fumbled for what seemed endless minutes before she figured out the lock, and finally flung the door open.

Cold air and snowflakes flooded in and swirled around her. Smoke surged from the fireplace, and Delainey grabbed the plastic that had been wrapped around the firewood and tried desperately to fan the fumes toward the door.

A shadow loomed in the doorway. "What in the hell are you doing? Trying to burn the whole place down?"

It was the cretin-next-door, still in the faded jeans but without the leather jacket. Instead he was wearing a sweatshirt with the sleeves pushed to the elbows. And his voice no longer sounded like cashmere but more like canvas—rough and abrasive.

Just what I need.

At the moment, however, Delainey was desperate enough to accept help from any source. "The fire just flared up all of a sudden," she said. "I got all the plastic off the wood, I'm sure of it, so I don't know why it's smoking like that."

He glanced at the fireplace, shot a look at her, and set her briskly out of his way as he headed for the kitchen. Over his shoulder, he said, "Of course it didn't occur to you before you lit the fire that a poker would be a useful thing to have on hand."

Delainey bit her lip. There was no sense in answering something that so obviously hadn't been intended as a question.

Drawers rattled, paper rustled, and she heard a muttered curse. Then he came back with her silver sugar tongs in his hand and dropped to his knees by the fireplace.

Delainey put out a hand to stop him. "You can't use those! That's *silver*—"

"Watch me." The tongs gleamed red in the firelight as he reached over the flames, up into the chimney, and pulled. There was a metallic thud, and he sat back on his heels.

The air was still thick and gray, but instead of rolling into the room now, the smoke was going up the chimney.

"A fireplace works better when you open the damper before you strike the match," he said.

"I guess I should have known that." Delaney watched as he patted out a spark which had settled on the front of the sweatshirt. "I hope you didn't get burned."

"Singed the hair on my arms a little." He stood up. "Those bundles of so-called firewood are pretty useless— and that's a good thing. If the wood hadn't been dry as cardboard, you'd have had smoke so thick you'd have had to knock a hole in the roof to vent it."

He was right about the firewood, Delainey realized. The blaze was already dying down; the half-dozen sticks were little more than embers. It hadn't even been a hot enough blaze to melt the few snowflakes that still clung to his hair.

"Thanks," she said. " I'm sorry for yelling at you about the tongs. And I'll replace the sweatshirt."

"No need. It's been exposed to worse things than

sparks.'' He handed the tongs to her. ''Don't close the damper till the fire's completely out.''

She nodded, but she was thinking, *As if I'm actually going to touch that fireplace ever again!*

''Is there anything else you'd like me to do for you?'' he said pleasantly.

Delainey bit her lip as she recognized her own words quoted back at her. ''No, I think that takes care of it.'' What had he said his name was? Wagner, that was it. ''Thanks again, Mr. Wagner.''

''Sam,'' he said.

''What?''

''It's just a quirk of mine, but I think a lady who entertains in her pajamas should be on a first name basis with her guests.''

Delainey gritted her teeth and brushed feebly at a sooty streak on her satin sleeve.

He smiled and turned toward the French door. ''Want me to close this, or are you planning to just stand in here and freeze?''

Damn the man; he had the memory of a tape recorder. ''I think I'll let the place air out a little more first.'' She looked down at the silver tongs in her hand, now smudged with smoke, and added tentatively, ''Honestly, I'm not incompetent in general. Just inexperienced with fireplaces.''

''Well, that's good,'' Sam said. ''Because I was really starting to worry about what might happen when you tried to take a shower.''

He was whistling as he crossed the patio toward his own back door.

I'm buying a poker tomorrow, Delainey thought. *But not for the fireplace. Just so I'll have it handy to use as a murder weapon.*

The doorbell rang as Delainey was coming down the stairs the next morning, still tightening an earring. She peeked out to see a woman on the doorstep, every gray hair in place and a basket in her hand.

"Welcome to the neighborhood," the woman said when Delainey opened the door. "My name's Emma Ashford and I live right around the corner." She held out the basket. "Muffins for your first breakfast in your new home. Actually, I tried to leave some for you last night, but your moving men seemed to think I was taking pity on them and by the time I'd explained, they'd cleaned up every crumb."

Delainey inhaled the rich fragrance of vanilla and cinnamon which rose from the folds of the napkin which lined the basket. "So you baked these this morning? I'll have to thank the moving men for being greedy, because I get muffins straight from the oven.... Won't you come in?"

Emma hesitated. "I don't mean to be a pest. I know you working girls keep a ferocious schedule."

"Actually, I have all the time in the world this morning, because I'm stuck here while I wait for a delivery." Delainey led the way to the kitchen. "Coffee?"

"Only if you're making some for yourself."

"It's no trouble at all." Delainey took two plates from the cabinet. One was white plastic with fake gold trim; the other was blue pottery. "Not very elegant, I'm afraid. China that actually matched was never a priority when I shared an apartment."

"Of course not. Roommates can be so careless." Emma settled herself at the breakfast bar and began to unpack the basket. "This most be your first real home."

Delainey nodded and ran a finger across the rough surface of the counter where the previous owner's hot skillet had damaged it. "It'll be a while before I get it all into shape."

"It always takes twice as long as you expect, and three times as much money."

"Oh, that's a comfort," Delainey said dryly. She

plugged the coffeepot in and reached into the cabinet for a pair of mismatched mugs. "Did you know the previous owners?"

"Not well. I've only been here a short while myself." Emma split a muffin and set it on the blue pottery plate, pushing it across the breakfast bar to Delainey.

Delainey wanted to ask why she was living there at all. White Oaks was hardly a retirement community; from what Patty had told her, the average age of the residents was about thirty. But she couldn't think of a way to phrase the question without sounding rude, so she turned her attention back to the coffeepot, which didn't seem to be doing anything.

"That's odd," she muttered. "It was all right when I used it a couple of days ago." She moved it to the other side of the sink and plugged it into a different outlet, and it immediately began to swish and sigh. "Oh, that's great— a dead outlet, too, right in the middle of the kitchen. Maybe I can get an electrician to come while I'm waiting around anyway."

"The same day you call? Unlikely."

"I suppose you're right. Will you excuse me for just a minute? I need to call the bank so my boss knows I won't be in till late."

"If it's just a package you're waiting for, the clubhouse manager will be happy to sign for it and keep it till you get home."

"Actually, it's a bed." Delainey glanced across the living area at the futon where—she hoped—she had spent her last night ever. "A whole bedroom set, in fact. It was supposed to be delivered first thing this morning, but the department store called just before you got here to say the truck would be delayed."

"What a nuisance. There's no telling when they'll actually show up."

"That's what I'm afraid of," Delainey said glumly. "I

really can't afford to take the time off, because I just started this job six weeks ago.''

''You said you work for a bank?''

''National City. I'm in the business-loan division.''

''Then we certainly can't have you being late,'' Emma said briskly. ''You go on to work—after you've finished your muffin, of course—and I'll keep an eye out for the deliverymen.''

''That would be lovely, but I can't ask you to—''

''You didn't ask. I offered. That's what neighbors do.''

''Not the kind of neighbors I've ever had before,'' Delainey said. She surveyed Emma Ashford more closely. Con artist? Nosy old woman? Neither, she concluded. Emma was just a nice lady who was probably a bit lonely in this community of younger people, and who had a little too much time on her hands.

Delainey had encountered dozens of women like Emma Ashford during her years at the teller's window. In a backward sort of way, she'd be doing Emma a favor in letting her help—though nothing like the magnitude of the favor Emma was doing for her.

''Just show me which bedroom.'' Emma stood up. ''And I'll take care of the rest.''

Almost everything about Delainey's job was new. The promotion had taken her to a higher level of responsibility, with a new title and a new boss, and a new office that was an actual room, not just a cubicle. For the first time in her career she had both a door and a secretary. Delainey hadn't yet decided which thrilled her more—running a fingertip across the silvery doorplate with her name engraved on it, or having Josie keeping track of the calls she needed to return and the appointments on her calendar.

When she came in, Josie was printing the day's appointments list, and she passed it across the desk. ''It's already outdated, though. Mr. Bishop wants to see you in his office right away.''

Bless Emma Ashford, Delainey thought. Without the woman's offer, she'd have been sitting at home waiting on a delivery truck instead of being here to answer the boss's summons. And since it was the first time in a week that she'd done more than exchange greetings with him in the hallway, it would have been a particularly bad day to have been late.

Delainey gathered up the projects she'd been working on and crossed the hall to the corner office with its view of the downtown skyline. Someday, perhaps, this view would be hers...

She squashed the thought before it could get out of hand. *Concentrate on the job you've already got,* she reminded herself, *and the next promotion will take care of itself.* It was a philosophy that hadn't led her astray in the ten years since she'd first sat behind a teller's window as a trainee, too nervous about the sheer size of the piles of cash she was handling to worry about anything else. ''RJ? You wanted to see me?''

RJ Bishop ran a hand through his heavy, prematurely gray hair and waved her to an overstuffed chair across from his desk. ''Have a seat, Delainey. Time to catch up on what's been going on. How are you enjoying the job?''

''I love it, RJ. In fact, I have an idea to run by you when you have a minute.''

''No time like the present.''

Delainey took a deep breath. ''There are a lot of women in this town who have good ideas for small businesses, but they're having a lot of trouble getting started. I've been thinking about how we could set up a business incubator to help them out. They could have a good address and a private office, but they could share some of the more expensive resources for a while until they get on their feet.''

There was a tap on the door and another of the department's staff came in. "You wanted me, RJ?"

Delainey surveyed the newcomer with interest. She hadn't worked with Jason Conners before—had barely met him, in fact. When she joined the team, he'd been wrapping up the financing on a venture-capital deal that had kept him out of the office much of the time.

"Sit down, Jason." RJ looked at Delainey again. "A business incubator would be a pretty expensive proposition."

"Not necessarily. We'd charge rent, of course, and a percentage of the profits."

Jason hitched up his perfectly creased trousers and perched on the arm of the chair next to Delainey's. "If there are any profits."

Delainey turned to look him in the eye. "We'd have a high percentage of failures, yes, but one big success would more than make up for a dozen losses. Anyway, the gain for us would be much more than financial. The women who make their businesses work will be loyal to the bank because we gave them a hand when they needed it. We'll have all their deposits and loans—and a great deal of goodwill, too."

"Women only?" Jason sniffed. "It's hardly worth the risk of being accused of discrimination, RJ."

I haven't missed much, not working with him, Delainey thought. "But I don't want to take up any more of Jason's valuable time with that discussion, RJ," she said smoothly. "We can talk about it later."

"Why?" Jason asked. "Afraid I'll poke holes in your reasoning?"

"Let's drop the incubator idea for now, Delainey, and move on to the Bannister deal." RJ leaned forward. "I want to bring Jason up to speed on what you've been doing with Elmer Bannister's numbers."

Delainey pulled the folder from her pile and showed him

the projections she'd done on how they could pull together the capital that Elmer Bannister needed in order to expand his factory.

RJ listened patiently, running a fingertip over the figures. Jason fidgeted.

Finally, RJ nodded. "It looks good," he said. "Bringing together Elmer Bannister's product and that particular group of investors. What do you think, Jason?"

Jason shrugged. "It's not bad. I'll call the investors and make the proposal."

"Excuse me," Delainey said. "*You'll* make the proposal? RJ, I put this together. I should be the one to—"

RJ was shaking his head. "Not this time, Delainey. You could probably pull it off, but—"

Darn right I could pull it off, Delainey thought irritably.

"But we don't want to risk your hard work by putting you on the front line like that just yet. You'll help Jason when he makes the presentation, get some experience that way."

While Jason takes the credit. But Delainey knew that further argument would get her nowhere. "Yes, sir."

RJ grinned at her. "I think that's all then. I'll let you two work out the details." He pulled his chair up to the desk and reached for a pen.

Dismissed, Delainey gathered up her folders. Jason ostentatiously held the door for her.

As if I'm such a little feminine flower that I couldn't manage to pull it open for myself. She started down the hall.

"Delainey," Jason said. "A word of warning. RJ likes his people to be a team. So the question is, are you a team player?"

She didn't look at him. "I've never had a problem working in groups, Jason."

"Good. Then you'll be eager to be a part of the next deal I'm working on. Heard of Curtis Whittington?"

''Hasn't everybody? What's the merger king working on this time?''

Jason laughed. ''Cute nickname—but I'd suggest you not call him that to his face when we have lunch with him tomorrow.''

''He's in town?''

''Well, we're not having lunch by conference call. Unless you'd rather not be on the team?''

Delainey kept her voice calm. ''I don't have any other plans.''

Jason laughed. ''That's what I thought. Century Club, one o'clock. In the meantime, do your homework.''

He strolled off down the hall, leaving Delainey chewing her bottom lip and wondering whether he was setting her up or offering her the chance of a lifetime.

Her secretary spent half the afternoon at the library, and Delainey went home a little early but with a briefcase stuffed to bursting with reading material about Curtis Whittington. Too bad she'd sworn off fires, she thought absently. It would be pleasant to sit beside a blaze tonight with a glass of wine, reading her way through the stack of magazines Josie had culled.

For an instant when she pulled up in front of the town house complex, she thought she had been caught in a time warp and flung back to the previous day. A big truck was parked in front, and two burly men were coming down the sidewalk. But it wasn't a moving van this time, just a delivery truck from the department store. ''Everything's in but the bedside tables,'' one of them called as she got out of her car. ''We'll be done in a minute.''

''I thought you were supposed to be here this morning.''

''Oh, it worked out better to reverse the deliveries,'' the man said cheerfully.

''Better for whom?'' Delainey said under her breath. Not for Emma Ashford, that was certain. Poor woman, casually offering to do a good deed that she expected would take an hour or two at most, and then having to wait around all day....

There was one good thing about it as far as Delainey was concerned, though. She wouldn't have any trouble tracking Emma down to give her the flowers she'd brought as a thank-you gesture.

She gathered up the sheaf of pink roses and her bulging briefcase and followed a pair of bedside tables up the sidewalk. Coming in out of the sunlight, she blinked in the sudden dimness inside the town house. For a minute all she could distinguish was movement in the kitchen.

"Emma?" she called. "I can't thank you enough for—"

But as her eyes adjusted, she saw that it wasn't Emma in the kitchen. It was the cretin-next-door, and he seemed to be making himself right at home.

Sam Wagner looked up. "Flowers?" he said gently. "For me? Oh, honey—you shouldn't have!"

CHAPTER TWO

DELAINEY stormed across the big room and set her brief-case on the breakfast bar. The magazines she'd stuffed in-side slid out and cascaded across the counter and onto the floor. "What are *you* doing in my house?"

"At the moment," Sam said, "I'm wiring in a new out-let. But if you object, I can stop."

Her gaze dropped to his hands. His long fingers moved quickly and with a grace that surprised her, winding a pair of colored wires together and twisting a plastic cap over the joint.

She'd forgotten all about the outlet. Emma must have told him it needed repairing—but why? "Are you an elec-trician?"

"Not exactly, so don't tell the union I'm fiddling with wires." He fitted the outlet back into the box in the wall and reached for a screwdriver to fasten it in place.

"Then…are you the maintenance man for the com-plex?" That made sense, Delainey thought. With a hundred units on the estate, it would certainly be a full-time job to keep up with minor repairs for all the residents. And having a handyman living right on site would be a good idea, too, because he'd be able to respond faster in an emergency.

The use of a town house might be a part of his pay— and a job like that would certainly explain Sam Wagner's faded jeans and sweatshirt and running shoes. A mainte-nance man never knew what messes his day might include. Though today, she noted, he was wearing khakis and a pullover sweater. *He's positively dressed up.*

"Not officially."

Delainey felt like stamping her foot. "Then what are you?"

"You sound so suspicious that I'd rather not admit to anything." Sam gave a last twist to the mounting screw and put the plastic protective plate back in place over the outlet. "There. It should be as good as new." He gathered up bits of wire and insulation and dumped them in the trash can. "Well, now that you're here to supervise the delivery team, I'll just take my flowers home and get them into water."

Reminded of the roses, Delainey clutched the bouquet a little tighter. "Is Emma upstairs?"

"No. Why? You're afraid the deliverymen couldn't set up the bed without her advice? Though it *is* quite a bed, I must say. Even the deliverymen must not see one like that very often."

"Of course you would have to go take a look," she said irritably. "I hope you satisfied your curiosity."

Sam shrugged. "I wasn't being nosy."

"Oh, no, of course not!"

"I was just doing my job as a supervisor, keeping a close eye on things. I'd hate to have you come home and find out they'd put it together upside down or something."

"The real question is why you were supervising at all. What happened to Emma?"

"Bridge club, every Tuesday afternoon at the mansion. When the delivery people didn't show up on time, she saddled me with the job and went off to play cards." He began gathering up tools. "You must have been sleeping on a futon for a long time to make you go all out like that when you bought a real bed."

Delainey willed herself not to blush. How she chose to furnish her bedroom was certainly none of his business. "She left you here alone?"

"You're complaining? She could have just put a note on the door telling the delivery people to try again tomorrow."

And since it wasn't Emma's bed, Delainey reminded herself, who would blame her for setting limits on her Good Samaritan offer? "I'm not complaining exactly. Just surprised, since she said she'd take care of it."

"I know." Sam nodded thoughtfully. "You'd think by the time a woman hits seventy-five, she'd learn to be responsible for doing what she says she's going to. On the other hand, now you have your outlet fixed too." He opened a yellow plastic case and began to fit tools into the slots and crevices inside. "Maybe you should go up and make sure they're doing things right."

Maybe she should, Delainey thought, because with any luck, he'd be gone by the time she came back down.

"Don't forget to stomp your feet on the stairs to warn them—just in case they've been trying on your lingerie up there."

She pretended not to hear him. "The outlet—what do I owe you for your work?"

His eyes brightened. "You mean you'll pay me as well as bring me flowers?"

"I can't imagine you wanting the flowers." She opened the cabinet where her skimpy supply of dishes resided and got out a big, heavy glass mug. "I'll stick them in water till Emma gets home. Which unit is hers?"

"She didn't tell you?"

"She just said she lived around the corner."

"Well, she does, sort of. That corner." He pointed.

"What? That's where you live. Wait a minute—you mean you and *Emma*—? No."

"If you'd like to be precise, she's my maternal grandmother."

Delainey flipped a switch to turn on the light over the sink. Nothing happened. "Oh, great. You've messed up the rest of the wiring!"

"No, I just pulled the breaker so I wouldn't electrocute myself while I worked."

"More's the pity," she said under her breath. She filled the mug and with difficulty fitted in the bunch of stems.

Sam casually shook a finger at her. "Just for that remark, I should make you turn the power back on yourself. No, on second thought, I'll do it. Before you ever touch the electrical system, I want to be at a safe distance. Easter Island *might* be far enough."

Delainey wasn't listening. "You live with your grandmother?"

"Last time I looked, it wasn't a crime."

"Aren't you just a little old for that? And this is two days in a row you've been hanging around here in the afternoon… Are you on vacation or what?"

"Extended," he said crisply.

There was something about his tone of voice that puzzled her for a moment. "Oh. You've been laid off? I'm sorry."

Sam nodded. "Downsized. Given the pink slip. Axed. Made redundant. Shown the door. Have you ever noticed how many ways we have to describe losing a job?"

"Fired," Delainey added helpfully.

"I was *not* fired."

"Sorry. I was just playing the game. I've never actually been out of work, but—"

"Very lucky for you."

"I know. I've been with the bank for ten years now. But I do understand how it affects a person to lose a job—it can be like losing his identity."

"Oh, I'm not at that stage yet," Sam said absently. "I still recognize myself in the mirror when I shave."

Why bother to waste compassion on the man? "Well, good luck finding something to do."

"Gran's keeping me busy. Everybody she knows has something that needs fixed."

That wasn't what Delainey had meant, but she decided not to press the point. It would be no wonder if Emma Ashford was trying her best to keep her grandson occupied.

Having a grown man lying about the house all day would get old in a hurry.

Sam crossed the kitchen to the pantry closet and moved aside half a dozen cans of condensed soup so he could reach the electrical panel at the back. "Good thing you haven't stocked up the shelves," he said. "Why they always put these things in the darkest and most inaccessible spot is beyond me."

There was a click from the direction of the closet, and abruptly the light over the sink glared straight into Delainey's eyes. Feeling a bit obstinate, she plugged the toaster into the outlet he'd repaired and pushed the lever down.

"What's the matter? You didn't think I could do it?" He leaned both elbows on the breakfast bar.

Inside the toaster, the coils glowed red. She unplugged it. "I was just making sure. So that's what you meant earlier about not being the official handyman around here. Emma has you lined up as the *unofficial* one."

"It keeps me out of trouble."

Delainey had her doubts that any kind of job could accomplish that goal. "Well, thank you. Let me know what I owe you for the work."

Sam picked up the last of the tools. "Oh, I couldn't charge a fee."

"Why on earth not?" She was so intrigued she forgot she was still holding the toaster. "Seriously, Sam, this could be a nice little business. There must be a huge demand for someone who'll do the little jobs that regular contractors don't want to bother with—things like broken outlets and drippy faucets and loose door handles."

"If that's a polite way to ask me to fix your drippy faucet and your loose door handle—"

"I haven't got any—at least none I've found yet. I was speaking generally. You wouldn't need much to get started. Just business cards, a nicely printed fee schedule, some advertising, a phone number and a reliable answering service.'' She eyed the fitted case with its neat but limited assortment of screwdrivers and pliers. It was definitely an amateur's kit, the kind of thing she'd have to buy for herself sometime soon. ''You'll need some better tools, of course, and maybe a truck or a van.''

''And the necessary licenses and permits. I wasn't kidding about the electricians' union.'' He closed the toolbox with a click that sounded almost final.

''Oh. I hadn't thought of that. But getting the money to start shouldn't be a problem. I'll help you put together a business plan and a loan application.'' She delved into her briefcase, scooping out the few magazines which hadn't already escaped when she set it down, and pulled out a gold case engraved with her initials. ''Here's my card. We do this kind of thing all the time.''

He took the bit of glossy paper and looked at it thoughtfully. ''Delainey Hodges, Business Loan Officer, National City Bank.''

''Think it over and call me.''

He tapped a finger against the card. ''Do you always make loans so impulsively?''

She was annoyed. ''Look, Sam, I didn't promise to back this enterprise.''

''It certainly sounded to me like that's what you were doing. Do you get paid based on how many loans you can talk people into taking?''

''I just think it would be a great idea. And I didn't guarantee you a loan, I said I'd help you apply for financing. If the package looked good, then the bank would probably be happy to give you a loan.''

''I don't doubt it. The criteria seems to be if the client can prove he doesn't need the money, the bank will lend it.'' He put her business card in his pocket.

''That's not the way it works. What happened to put you

off banks, anyway?'' she asked shrewdly. ''Did somebody repossess your car after you lost your job, or what?''

He didn't answer, but flicked a fingertip across Curtis Whittington's face on the cover of a financial magazine. ''Unless it's somebody like this, of course. Then the bigger the loan amount and the riskier the ride, the happier the bank is to help out.'' The magazine slid a little, showing that Whittington's face was on the one underneath as well. Sam's eyebrows rose. ''Are you a fan?''

''Of the merger king? Not exactly. But I'm having lunch with him tomorrow.''

''Lucky you. Do you want me to take the flowers?''

''No, I'll bring them over later. When did you say Emma will be home?''

''About six. My feelings are hurt, you know. What did Gran do to deserve flowers?''

''Hey, I offered to pay you. Twice.''

''I remember. I'll let you know when I figure out what kind of reimbursement I can accept without losing my amateur standing. Of course, there's always—''

Delainey tried to swallow a gasp. *He's only jerking your chain,* she told herself.

''Though maybe it's not worth the risk,'' he said earnestly. ''If you could cook, your pantry wouldn't be so empty.''

She was too startled to stay silent. ''You were going to ask me to *cook* something for you? Not—'' She noticed that his deep blue eyes were starting to sparkle like moonlight on a lake, and swallowed hard.

''I'm always willing to listen to an offer,'' Sam said gently. ''What sort of currency did you have in mind?''

''Nothing.''

''Right. Well, I'll keep thinking. I'm sure I'll come up with something.''

''Don't twist your brain into knots over it.''

Sam smiled. ''I'll tell Gran you're going to stop by.

She'll be pleased—she was making noises earlier today about giving you a housewarming party.''

"That's lovely of her, but—''

"Yes, isn't it thoughtful? I already know what I'm going to get you.''

Delainey couldn't stop herself. "What?'' she asked warily.

"An accessory for the next time you use your fireplace.''

"If you're thinking of buying me a poker, I should warn you—''

"Nothing so dull. I'm going to get you a smoking jacket, so you won't have to keep ruining your pajamas. See you later, sweetheart.''

Sam had left the garage door open when he'd gone over to Delainey's to rescue Emma, so it was easy to put the tool kit back on the shelf on his way through.

Delainey had been right on target about one thing, he thought as he lined the plastic box up precisely with the dust-free outline it had left on the metal shelf. But it was one he hadn't expected she would pick up on at all.

You'll need some better tools, of course, she'd said almost casually. And she was right—he'd practically twisted the head off one of the cheap screwdrivers just putting that outlet back together. But he hadn't expected that she'd know the difference.

The woman might not be able to light a fire, but at least there were a few practical bits of knowledge floating around under all that shiny gold-flecked hair. And a good thing it was, too, because if she was going to hard-sell business loans, she'd better know what she was talking about.

And that had definitely been a hard sell she'd given him. For a minute there, Sam had half expected to find himself in the home-repair business without ever having had a chance to refuse. Scarier yet was the fact that the longer she'd talked, the more it had started to sound like a good idea.

Of course, loaning the money to set up a small home-repair business was a far different proposition from dealing with Curtis Whittington. The merger king, she'd called him. The merger maniac was more like it.

He wondered if Delainey was trying to hard-sell Curtis Whittington, or if things were the other way around.

The exterior trim on every single town house at White Oaks was basically the same, and the homeowner's covenant that Delainey had signed along with her down-payment check made it clear that it was to remain that way. No extra awnings, purple shutters, or odd-shaped mailboxes were allowed, and Delainey suspected if a pink plastic flamingo appeared on a front lawn that a note from the manager would soon follow, giving the bird instructions to migrate.

"There's a thought," she mused. If Sam Wagner got to be too annoying, she could line his driveway with neon-colored pinwheels and park a painted plaster statue of a jockey next to the front door. But of course it wouldn't be Sam who would have to take the nasty call from the complex manager, it would be Emma.

So much for a good idea.

Somehow, despite the rule about individualizing the town houses, Emma Ashford's stood out as more personal than the units Delainey drove past on her way in and out of the complex. A potted pine tree covered with red bows stood off to the side of the front door, a holly wreath hung above the bell, and at her feet a welcome mat decorated with Santa's face proclaimed "Welcome Ho-Ho-Home."

Delainey rang the bell and sighed at the reminder that Christmas was only three weeks away. It wasn't that she was a Scrooge, but exactly when was she going to find time to search out her few Christmas decorations, much less to put them up?

Emma ushered her inside, exclaimed over the roses, and went to put them in water. As Delainey waited for her to finish, she looked around. This town house was larger than her own, though the plan of the first floor was similar— basically one huge room divided into various living areas. The main difference was that the kitchen was separated by a wall rather than just a breakfast bar.

The overall impression was of vibrant color—an unusual combination of purple, lavender, and hunter green. Delainey was a little surprised, because the brilliant colors didn't quite seem Emma's style. She would have expected old-fashioned floral chintz that had faded gently over time until only the softest tones were left. But hadn't Emma said something about not having lived at White Oaks long herself? Maybe she'd gone for all new furniture when she moved.

Considering the welcome mat and the wreath outside, she was also startled that there was no Christmas tree to be seen. But perhaps Emma was a purist about having a live tree and was just waiting till closer to the holiday to put it up.

On the back of a wing chair near the fireplace, a seal-point Siamese cat yawned and sat up, and deep blue eyes inspected Delainey from head to toe. "Well, hello there," she said, holding out a hand for the cat to sniff.

Sam came down the stairs in the worn leather jacket with a helmet under his arm. "I see you've already met the Empress," he said.

"Is that her name?"

"Not even close. Her official name is some long, involved, incredibly complicated mix of Oriental-sounding vowels. I gave up on it a long time ago, and she's just been the Empress ever since. Was Gran suitably impressed with the flowers?"

"She seemed to like them."

"I still think you should have given them to me instead.

She gets flowers all the time, so it doesn't have the same impact on her as it would on me."

"That," Emma said from the doorway, "is nothing more than slander. I adore roses and these are particularly lovely ones. And they're always more fun when they're a surprise."

"As they are this time, because you didn't do anything to earn them." Sam grinned at her. "I was the one working my head off while you were over at the clubhouse going no trump and letting the manager wait on you hand and foot."

"He's very nice to us," Emma admitted. "Have you met the manager, Delainey?"

"Not yet. In fact, I've never been in the mansion. I was so short of time the day I looked at the town house that I didn't get any further."

"Well, you definitely need to do something about that," Emma said. "The mansion is one of the best features of the whole complex—it has a little of everything. Are you going out, Sam?"

"I'm not just polishing my helmet, Gran."

"Well, have a good time," Emma said.

Delainey watched as Sam set the helmet on his head. "You ride a motorcycle? Wait a minute—then why were you so fussed yesterday about the moving van blocking the drive? You could have gotten past it easily."

"On the motorcycle, yes. But I was putting Gran's car away." He fastened the chin strap and tightened it.

"Where were we?" Emma asked. "Oh, yes—the clubhouse facilities. You should go over for dinner, at least, Delainey."

"It wouldn't be much fun to go alone," Delainey said. "Perhaps you'll be my guest."

"She gets flowers *and* dinner?" Sam muttered.

Though he sounded hurt, Delainey was willing to bet he was trying to smother amusement instead of woe.

Emma shot a disapproving look at him. "The boy has no manners, of course—but he's right. He did do all the work."

Now there was no question; Sam's eyes—even bluer than those of the Siamese—were full of humor. The cretin was laughing at her.

Still, even though Delainey felt she'd been set up by an expert, there was only one graceful thing to do. "I meant both of you, of course," she said.

"And anyone who believes that," Sam said under his breath, "is due for a serious reality check."

Delainey raised her voice just a little. "How unfortunate that Sam has other plans so he can't accompany us."

"Then we'll go tomorrow," Emma said comfortably. "Going on Wednesday night will be better anyway. There's always live entertainment on Wednesdays, and that usually means a crowd. You'll be able to meet some of the neighbors."

By the time that Delainey ushered her last client of the morning out of her office, her secretary was practically vibrating with anxiety. *You're late,* she mouthed behind the client's back. Delainey waved a hand to acknowledge her and went right on talking to the client.

The instant the woman was gone, Josie bounced out of her chair and seized Delainey's coat from the tiny closet. "You can't be late to the Century Club."

"It isn't that special, surely." Delainey slid into her coat.

"Yes, it is. I went to a wedding there once—well, a sort of bridal show thing. It's not only beautiful, but the waiters do everything just so. Twelve forks at every place—"

"Surely not."

"Maybe not twelve," Josie conceded. "But it's very fancy. Hurry—Mr. Conners said he'd be in the lobby at half-past twelve, and it's almost that now. You can't keep him waiting."

I'd like to, Delainey thought. She shoved her scarf in a pocket, because Josie was looking as if she'd like to grab hold and tie it herself. *As if she wants me to make a good impression when I go out to play with the other kids.*

Jason Conners wasn't in the lobby. Delainey wasn't surprised; she had half expected him to be late even though he was the one who'd set the time, because he seemed the sort who enjoyed making an entrance. So she leaned against the marble-topped reception desk to wait.

Five minutes went by, and she was just starting to think about walking back down the hall to check whether he was still in his office when she heard her name called.

But it wasn't Jason Conners who was walking toward her across the lobby. It was Sam, and he was coming in the main entrance. "Is it part of your job to stand there and be decorative?" he asked as he approached. "I thought banks had budgets for stuff like art."

Delainey let her eyebrows creep up. "Thank you for saying I'm ornamental. However, if you're flattering me because you've come to talk about your loan—"

"I wouldn't do that."

"Flatter me at all, or flatter me to get a loan? Never mind. You've got about two minutes, tops, to make your case."

"Before you have to leave for lunch with the merger king? Sorry to disappoint you, but I came in to cash a check for Gran. However, I've been thinking about that loan."

There was a note of idle humor in his voice that made Delainey brace herself.

"I've figured out why you're so determined to give it to me—you need just one more loan in your portfolio in order to be named employee of the month and win a trip to Hawaii. So I'm willing to talk about terms."

"I suppose your terms include that I take you along to Hawaii?"

"Of course. It would be only fair, if I help you win."

"Well, that makes sense," Delainey admitted. "And I'd think very hard about it—*if* we had an employee of the month contest and *if* the prize was a trip to Hawaii. It's just too bad for you the bank doesn't run promotions like that."

"Want me to go talk to the president about it?" He checked his wristwatch. "I have a few minutes to kill, and I'm sure he'd like the idea. I might have it fixed by lunchtime."

"Thanks, anyway, Sam, but I think you should stick to fixing things like outlets."

A hand came to rest on her shoulder and Jason Conners said, "I've just talked to Curtis—he can't make lunch. Something came unglued in some big deal he's working on and he's tied up for a while. But we scheduled dinner instead."

Nice of you to ask me first whether it would be convenient, Delainey thought. But she said, "Still at the Century Club? What time?"

"No—he said he's been there so often he's tired of it. I was telling him about you, and when he heard you lived at White Oaks, he said he'd like to try it for a change. Apparently the place has a wider reputation than I thought." He looked Delainey over speculatively, as if trying to figure out how she'd managed to beat him to a trend. "That's all right with you, isn't it? Arrange it for eight o'clock. And wear something…attractive." His gaze slid over Sam and dismissed him as unimportant. Then he patted Delainey's shoulder and strode off down the hall toward the loan department.

"Nice guy," Sam said.

Of course he would have to be there to witness the whole thing, Delainey thought irritably. "Well, I don't imagine you were best buddies with everyone you ever worked with. Or is that why you're not working right now? Because you couldn't get along with the people you didn't like?"

Sam seemed not to hear her. "You're a business loan

officer *and* his secretary," he said admiringly. "You're one busy woman."

"Put a sock in it, Sam. Tell Emma we'll have dinner another time, all right?"

"You're standing us up? I've heard some fancy excuses to get out of a dinner date in my day, but this one—"

"You've heard excuses?" Delainey deliberately let a note of wonder creep into her voice. "You mean *personally?* There have actually been women who didn't fall all over themselves to get a date with you?"

Sam's lower lip quivered in the best imitation of a scolded three-year-old that Delainey had ever seen. "You have a mean streak that runs all the way through, Delainey."

"And you don't? That crack about me being a secretary… Tell Emma I'm sorry to disappoint her. I'll make it up to her."

"And to me, too?" Sam murmured. "Because I'm warning you—this time I'm going to hold out for a lot more than just roses."

Josie looked horrified when Delainey came back into the office, but when she heard what had happened she swung efficiently into action. "Don't worry about a thing, I'll make all the arrangements," she said, and she'd picked up the phone before Delainey could answer.

Delainey, still not used to having someone else taking care of details, had to bite her tongue to keep from saying that she'd rather do it herself. But that, she knew, would hurt Josie's feelings, so she went back into her office and buried herself in the paperwork for a new loan application.

Still, she couldn't quite put the whole thing out of her mind. It wasn't Josie, after all, who would immediately face the music from Jason Conners if they ended up with a table next to the kitchen door. It was Delainey who would face

Jason's scorn, and she'd already had enough of that to last her a while.

She was sure that Josie would do her level best, but some things were out of Josie's control. Emma had said that Wednesday nights were always busy at the mansion—and even if the manager recognized Delainey's name as a new tenant, he didn't know anything about her yet, so he probably wouldn't go out of his way. Of course the established customers would get preference.

She arrived at the Mansion early so she could check on the arrangements, and the manager greeted her with a smile. "Ms. Hodges," he said. "Everything is ready."

Delainey was startled. "How do you even know my name?"

"Well, partly because I make it a point to know all the tenants, so a new face stands out. But Mr. Wagner stopped earlier to make sure you got extra-special treatment."

That's downright terrifying, Delainey thought. She was morally certain that Sam's notion of extra-special wasn't the same as her own.

"Would you like to see which table he suggested for you?" Without waiting for an answer, the manager led the way to the dining room.

She was so early that the only people in the room were the busboys who were putting the finishing touches on the tables and in one corner an older couple who were already eating their soup. The manager showed Delainey to a table set for three. It was probably the best location in the room, near a huge marble fireplace where a gas fire flickered, but not so close that the heat would be excessive.

That probably hadn't been Sam's reason for choosing it, however, Delainey thought. He'd no doubt figured that if she was any closer to the flames, she'd manage to set herself ablaze.

She could see nothing wrong with any of the arrangements, but that didn't entirely relieve her apprehension as she sat at the library bar, toying with a glass of wine while she waited for Curtis Whittington and Jason to arrive.

She tried to distract herself by studying the room. So this was where Emma had been playing bridge yesterday. It was a warm, pleasant room, with a high coffered ceiling and long walls lined with books—the kind which looked as if someone had actually read them. The soft strains of Mozart wafted in from the grand piano in the drawing room next door—the live entertainment that Emma had mentioned.

When Jason and Curtis arrived, Delainey slid off the bar stool to greet them. She was mildly surprised to see that Curtis Whittington looked older in person than he had on the magazine covers. But then, she reminded herself, the profiles she'd read last night had been uniformly complimentary about the merger king's magic touch in making the businesses he acquired more successful—so why would a magazine use a photograph that wasn't flattering?

In fact, however, Curtis not only looked older in person than in his portraits, but he looked older than he actually was. Though he was just past forty, his stooped shoulders and the deep-slashed lines in his face made him appear a decade more. He looked like a man with an enormous burden to bear.

If his business weighed so heavily on him, Delainey wondered, why didn't he chuck it and retire to enjoy the fortune he'd already made? Perhaps it simply hadn't occurred to him that he could stop the amusement-park ride and get off anytime he wanted. Or perhaps it was ego that kept driving him to the next even bigger deal.

She saw Jason point her out, but he hung back a bit as Curtis approached. Behind the merger king's back, Jason gestured toward Delainey's dress and made a thumbs-up gesture to her. It was enough to make her wish she'd ignored his heavy-handed suggestion and worn a business suit instead of the sleek black velour with its heart-shaped neckline and lace-trimmed sleeves.

Curtis Whittington seemed to appreciate the dress, however. His dark brown eyes devoured her. "You're Delainey," he said. His voice was lower and more gravelly than she'd expected. "It's a pleasure." His hand was cold, and it was all Delainey could do not to shiver and pull away from his touch.

It's cold outside, dummy, she told herself. *It's not like he's a corpse.*

Curtis took the bar stool next to hers. "Nice place," he said. "Do you like living here?"

Apart from a few neighbors... "I think I'm going to like it very much. I'm still getting settled and learning my way around."

Jason snapped his fingers at the bartender and gave an order. "Curtis is thinking of buying something locally."

Delainey was startled. "You mean you'd move here? You're based in Seattle now, aren't you?"

"Oh, I wouldn't move exactly," Curtis said. "But hotels are such a nuisance. If I'm going to spend any time in a place, I like having my own territory. And I foresee the possibility of spending a lot of time here."

"Then there must be several companies you're interested in acquiring," Delainey said.

"Companies...and other things."

"Curtis just bought Foursquare Electronics," Jason said.

"Yes, I read that." Delainey just hoped nobody quizzed her about it, since that was one of the magazine articles she hadn't had time to finish. "Are you looking to expand more in that direction, or new ones?"

"I'm always interested in something new," Curtis said, and winked.

The bartender brought the drinks, and Curtis knocked his Scotch back and ordered another before the man had even moved away.

Delainey regarded him thoughtfully. If the man continued to drink at that rate… ''Perhaps we should go on in to dinner.''

Jason shook his head. ''There's no hurry. Let's get to know each other.''

''We can get acquainted over dinner,'' Curtis said. ''Let's get started.''

While Delainey had been waiting in the library bar, the dining room had almost filled, and now only a few tables, including their own, stood empty. Here were all the new neighbors that—if this evening had gone as originally planned—she would be meeting right now, Delainey thought wistfully.

She glanced around the room and felt herself freeze. Now she knew what Sam's definition of extra-special treatment was. And she'd been right to be wary.

Because Sam and Emma had come to dinner after all— and they were sitting at the table next to hers.

CHAPTER THREE

DESPITE Delainey's effort at self-control, she must have gasped, because Jason's gaze focused sharply on her.

She knew she shouldn't have been surprised, because by now she'd had ample evidence of what Sam Wagner was capable of doing. Still, the idea that he would make a special effort to hang around and annoy her—as opposed to simply seizing an opportunity whenever it happened to conveniently present itself—was a little more than she could swallow.

Or perhaps she was being unfair, she told herself. He might have simply concluded that Emma shouldn't be cheated of her evening out...

More likely it was Emma's idea to come to dinner anyway, and Sam just decided to make the most of it.

At the next table, Emma looked up from her menu with a beatific smile and a casual little wave. She really was the perfect lady, Delainey thought—acknowledging an acquaintance but making it clear she didn't expect a conversation at the moment.

Sam, on the other hand, laid the wine list aside, turned halfway around in his chair, and said, "Well, hello there, Delainey."

"Always a pleasure to see you, Sam," Delainey murmured and deliberately chose the seat at their table which was farthest from him. Curtis practically fell over himself to hold the chair for her, and he seated himself next to her. Jason took the chair opposite Delainey's, on Curtis's other side.

"That's the guy who was with you in the bank today," Jason said.

Delainey was surprised; he hadn't seemed to pay enough attention to Sam that he'd have remembered him.

She let her gaze drift to the next table. It wasn't difficult to do without being obvious, because though she'd achieved the maximum possible distance from Sam, the chair she'd chosen meant that he was almost directly in her field of view.

He'd stopped twisting himself into a pretzel and turned back to face Emma, so Delainey could take her time looking him over. He was dressed more formally than she'd seen him before, in a plain dark blue shirt and an even-darker jacket, but no tie. She wondered if he owned one. Surely if he did, he'd have put it on—every other man in the room was wearing a tie, and a couple were even in tuxedos.

"I wouldn't have thought he was the sort to live here," Jason went on.

"You'd be surprised," Delainey murmured. "It seems to be a much more diverse complex than I originally thought."

"Then it's probably not what you're looking for, Curtis," Jason said.

"Oh, as long as most of the neighbors were as pleasant as Delainey here, I could overlook a few others." Curtis was looking around for the waiter.

Delainey noted his glass was empty once more. "The manager told me they had several particularly good appetizers on the menu tonight," she said. "Perhaps we should start with a selection." *And get some food into our distinguished guest before he makes a fool of himself.*

"Where is it you live again?" Curtis asked.

Delainey was momentarily at a loss. How could he possibly have forgotten? "Oh, you mean what area of the complex? My town house is only a couple of blocks from the mansion. It's between here and the gate, off to the north of the main drive."

"Maybe there's a unit you could look at, Curtis," Jason

suggested. "They must have one set up to show prospective buyers."

"Actually, I don't think they do," Delainey said. "It's not like a new development where you need a display home to look at because the one you're buying hasn't been finished yet. Here, having a town house set aside to show wouldn't make any sense, because it's only once in a while that a unit becomes available."

"There's a waiting list?" Curtis asked.

"Not officially, since it's not the management that sells them but the individual owners." Delainey asked the waiter to bring a platter of appetizers. "And of course that means they all look a little different on the inside anyway."

"But the floor plans are all the same," Jason objected.

"There are just a few different ones, that's true. Mine's a two-bedroom, but a couple of the other units in my building have three bedrooms."

"Well, that's the answer," Jason said. "You go look at Delainey's, Curtis, and then you'll know if you want one like it."

Curtis smiled broadly. "I'd love to come over after dinner, Delainey. Thanks for the invitation."

Not tonight's dinner, Delainey thought. *Sometime in the next century, perhaps.*

But she'd worry about that when the time came. The way things were shaping up, Curtis wouldn't be in any shape to pay visits by the time dessert rolled around, anyway. She settled for a noncommittal smile.

A sudden loud clang—it sounded like the opening bell of the New York Stock Exchange—made her jump.

Curtis reached into his pocket and pulled out a cell phone. The gesture was so smooth and practiced that it reminded Delainey of a gunfighter in an Old West movie. Perhaps he hadn't had quite as much to drink as she'd thought. Or maybe he was just very accustomed to handling large quantities of alcohol.

Now there's a scary thought.

Curtis barked a couple of orders into the phone, which made everybody at the surrounding tables look in their direction, and slammed it back in his pocket. "Damn aides can't take care of anything without someone holding their hands," he growled. The waiter set the platter of appetizers in the center of the table, and he scooped a pile of stuffed mushrooms onto his plate. "Oh—would you like one, Delainey? Let me get it for you."

"What's the problem?" Jason asked. "Another glitch in that acquisition you're working on?"

Delainey's mushroom started to slide off the serving spoon, and Curtis caught it between two fingers and maneuvered it to her plate. She studied the now-misshapen morsel and decided she'd rather eat weeds.

"If it's a problem with your financing," Jason said, "you know that wouldn't be happening if you had let us at National City put it together."

It was hardly the most subtle sales pitch in history, Delainey mused. But then Curtis Whittington wasn't exactly a subtle sort of guy—so maybe Jason knew exactly what he was doing.

"Yeah, yeah. We'll see." Curtis eyed Delainey's abandoned appetizer. "You don't like mushrooms?"

"Not particularly," she lied.

"Then let me get you something else."

She warded him off. "Thanks—I'll help myself." She groped for a topic that might keep the conversation going through dinner. "Curtis, I'd like to hear more about how you choose companies to acquire, and how the process works."

"Personally, I'd like to hear more about the Foursquare deal," Jason added.

"Maybe I'll tell you about it someday," Curtis said. "When it's all cooled down. There have been some other deals you might find interesting, Delainey. There was a plastics firm out in Seattle that I took over a year or two ago..."

Delainey tried to smother a sigh. It was shaping up to be a very long evening.

Delainey refused dessert without an instant's hesitation, but Jason ordered a slab of cake that looked like solid chocolate and worked his way slowly through it. Curtis drank brandy and told stories about his various business conquests, and Delainey counted the minutes.

Dinner couldn't possibly have dragged out as long as it seemed, for she couldn't help but notice that Emma and Sam were still at the next table, drinking coffee and chatting not only to each other but to other diners who stopped on their way through the room. How she wished she'd told Jason that she'd already made plans for this evening and she wasn't going to dinner with him and Curtis. What could he have done to her, anyway? He could hardly complain to RJ that she wasn't doing her job…

What a sad comment it is on the evening, she thought, *that you'd rather have spent it bickering with Sam Wagner!*

Jason savored another mouthful of chocolate and said, "That was a good one, Curtis. I guess you showed them you're not to be messed with."

"Not like I'm going to show some other people." The scrape of his chair warned Delainey that Curtis had moved closer. He set his brandy glass down and leaned toward her. "I'm not going to keep you waiting much longer now, Delainey," he said in a hoarse whisper. "If you're not finished with that cake soon, Jason, we're going to leave you behind."

"Go ahead," Jason said casually. "This is too good to waste. Tell you what, Curtis—you take Delainey home, and I'll just call a cab." He winked at Curtis. "That way I won't cramp your style, kids."

Curtis laughed.

Delainey was momentarily aghast—but only because Jason was being so flagrant. In truth, she wasn't surprised, because as she looked back, she could see that the entire evening had been shaping up this way, from the moment Jason had suggested she show Curtis her town house....

No, she realized, it had started even before then, clear back at the bank when Jason had set the time and suggested that she dress up. Now it was obvious why he'd included her in the first place—he'd intended from the beginning to use her as bait for Curtis Whittington. The only thing that had changed in the last few minutes was that he wasn't being coy about it anymore. He was looking very pleased with himself.

There was absolutely no doubt that Curtis had snapped up the bait. Add his drink-befuddled condition on top of an inexhaustible ego, and it was obvious that he was convinced Delainey couldn't wait to get him to herself. And Jason seemed to have concluded that Delainey was a willing lure.

The trouble was, with both of them pressing her, it was going to be a challenge to find a tactful way to break free. Even refusing a ride home was problematic, because it made so much sense for them to drop her off—they'd practically be driving past her front door.

Think like a diplomat, she told herself. *Screaming and running won't do.*

She played for time. "Oh, we'll wait for you to finish, Jason. There's no hurry, because I'll have to show you the town house some other day, Curtis. I'm afraid it's not in any condition to have company drop in tonight."

Jason frowned. "You can't back out now."

She looked him square in the eye. "You're the one who issued the invitation in the first place, Jason—not me. And it's simply not convenient for me to have guests tonight."

"What's the matter?" Jason sneered. "Is your roommate entertaining her boyfriend? At least that would explain how you're able to afford to live in a place like this."

Not a bad excuse, Delainey thought. *I should have thought of that one myself. Thanks, Jason.* "As a matter of fact—"

Curtis frowned. ''How badly do you want my business, Delainey?'' His voice was thick.

Not badly enough to take a drunken sot home with me, that's sure. Ah—there's the answer. It's exactly the approach that will discourage Curtis.

''I haven't even set up a bar yet,'' she said. ''So we'll have to do this some other time, Curtis, when I'll be able to offer you a drink.''

He frowned, but he seemed to accept her logic, riddled with holes though it was. Jason, she thought, would be more of a problem. He'd probably suggest that Curtis just take a bottle with him.

Jason was opening his mouth when a clear, deep, silky-smooth voice from the next table said, ''That's odd. I thought you worked for a bank, Delainey—but it's beginning to sound more like an escort service.''

Just what I wanted, she thought irritably. *Sam's help—if you can call it that.*

For a moment she couldn't even decide who was annoying her most—Jason the jerk, Curtis the wolf, or Sam the well-meaning meddler. On the whole, she thought, Sam took the prize.

Jason dropped his fork and twisted around. ''Who asked you to listen in, anyway?''

Sam looked him straight in the eye. Then he braced both hands on the edge of the table and pushed his chair back.

Delainey sucked in a deep breath. *It's too bad I never dreamed of being the cause of a duel,* she thought philosophically. *Because now's my big chance.*

But to her astonishment, Sam didn't throw a punch. He didn't even stand up. In fact, Delainey realized, he hadn't actually moved much more than an inch.

Nevertheless Jason sagged back into his seat as suddenly as if he'd been hammered by a left hook.

Her jaw dropped. No one elsewhere in the room could possibly have noticed anything going on, and yet she was as breathless as if she'd just watched a couple of boxers go ten rounds.

Curtis's eyes narrowed. "What business is it of yours?" he asked Sam. Suddenly his voice wasn't slurred anymore. He sounded absolutely sober.

Jason seemed to revive. "Yeah," he blustered. "Who asked you to butt in?"

Delainey noted that a ripple seemed to be spreading across the room; diners were turning to look curiously toward the scene by the fireplace. Though at the moment there was still nothing much for them to see—just three men frozen into position, Delainey thought, and a woman warily watching—that scenario was obviously not going to last long.

Nobody was going to back down—and the shock value of Sam's restraint was rapidly wearing off where Jason and Curtis were concerned. Any moment now one of them would make a move. Unless someone stepped in to defuse the situation, there would be blood on the carpet.

She assessed her surroundings. The manager was out of sight, probably unaware of the drama going on in the dining room. Delainey hadn't noticed Emma leaving the room, but she was nowhere to be seen either; there would be no help from that direction. So it was up to Delainey to take care of herself after all.

And, she thought, if she handled it just right, she could deflect Curtis Whittington *and* teach Sam Wagner that she was perfectly capable of taking care of herself without his interference—all in one easy step.

She laid one hand on Curtis's sleeve and stretched the other out toward Jason, palm out as if to say *stop*. "You'll have to excuse Sam, gentlemen," she said pleasantly. "He gets a little touchy sometimes where I'm concerned. Jason, Curtis—may I introduce my fiancé?"

Her fiancé? As in future husband?

For an instant, Sam felt as if he'd been kicked squarely

in the center of the stomach, but the shock dissipated almost instantly.

I asked for it, he told himself ruefully. And he ought to have seen it coming, too. Delainey had never shown any tendency to be slow off the mark—or, for that matter, hesitant to take care of herself. He probably shouldn't have intervened at all.

But sitting still, simply watching and listening while she extracted herself from the situation, wasn't his style. Besides, he hadn't liked the odds she was up against, or the stakes. And even a woman with excellent self-defense skills could use a hand now and then.

If deflecting her companions' attention onto himself would make it easier for her, then he'd take the heat. *Just nominate me for Mr. Fix-it.*

Well, he'd managed to deflect them all right. Both her co-worker and the merger king were now glaring at him as if he'd snatched their lollipops.

He could handle that. What worried him a bit was the gleam in Delainey's eyes. She'd obviously made that crackpot announcement for the sheer pleasure of watching him squirm, and it was just as apparent that she was looking forward to the payoff when he stumbled all over himself to deny it.

But that was where she was going to be disappointed.

He stood up, taking his time and keeping one eye on Delainey's co-worker—though he was pretty sure, despite the guy's bluster, that he wouldn't be throwing any punches. It was the merger maniac who required cautious handling. In his boozy state, Curtis might do anything at all.

Sam circled the table and bent over Delainey's chair. "It always makes me feel warm all over when you claim me like that," he said, his voice pitched just high enough to be certain that the two men at the table would catch every word. "You make it sound so sexy to be your fiancé." His lips brushed her cheekbone and moved slowly toward her mouth. Then, as if suddenly recalling the surroundings, he pulled back. "Come on, darling. Now that you're finally done with business, let's go home…and finish this in private."

Emma chatted gently on the short drive from the mansion to the town houses, while Delainey sat in the back of Emma's enormous old Cadillac and brooded. Sam was right about one thing, she told herself. They were going to finish things, that was sure.

And what exactly are you complaining about? a little voice in the back of her brain inquired. *You're upset because he played along—but that doesn't make any sense.*

He hadn't had to add fuel to the fire, though, she told herself.

"You'll be going over to Delainey's, of course," Emma said cheerfully as Sam shut the engine off. "Would you like me to leave the garage door open for you?"

"Thanks, Gran, but I've got my keys." He took Delainey's arm and ushered her out into the driveway. "Watch out, there's always a little patch of ice right there at the corner."

"This isn't going to take long," Delainey said through gritted teeth.

"Still, there's no need to stand out in the cold while we do the post-mortem. What a team we make—you never miss a cue, Delainey. Turning your head right into the kiss like that…and letting your eyes drift shut like you were mesmerized—you're good. Completely wasted in a banking career."

She remembered closing her eyes. But she'd swear she hadn't done anything so idiotic as turn her head to make it easier for him to kiss her. He was imagining things, and that made her feel peevish. "That was the most absurd display of primate behavior I've ever seen," she fumed. "I felt like I was in a chimpanzee cage."

Sam shrugged. "It worked, didn't it?"

"Don't flatter yourself. The whole thing was completely unnecessary. I've been in the business world for ten years, Sam, and I'm perfectly able to take care of myself—I don't need or want a man to step in and defend me."

"Perhaps I'm missing something here, but if you were so able to take care of yourself, why did you drag me into it?"

"*Drag* you? You volunteered."

"I'm not the one who announced the engagement."

"I was joking," Delainey said. "I was trying to break the tension, before the testosterone puddle got so deep somebody drowned in it!"

He said quietly, "You didn't look like it was a joke when the merger maniac was breathing on you and your co-worker was suggesting that you take customer service to an entirely new level. So don't expect me to believe that you were just playing a game."

Delainey's key slipped in her hand, and she tried without success to suppress the little shiver that ran over her.

"What were you going to do, Delainey? Accept the ride home and try to fight him off at the door?"

"Of course not. I wouldn't have gotten in a car with him. I'd have told him I had mine."

"And when he offered to walk you out to it, how would you have explained why it wasn't in the parking lot after all? And then what would you have done? Started off to stroll home? He'd have followed you—and you'd have been a sitting duck." Sam reached over her shoulder, turned the key, and opened the door.

Delainey stopped just inside, feeling the peace of the town house wash over her. Now that she was safe, she could no longer deny that the threat had been real. "No." Her voice caught just a little. "No, you're right. I was in a jam, and I appreciate you stepping in—even if it wasn't necessary."

"Not quite what I'd call a booming vote of thanks."

"It will have to do. Look, Sam, I'm sorry—the fiancé

line was a cheap shot to take at you, when all you were doing was trying to help. Can we just forget it ever happened?''

''We can try.'' He paused with one hand on the doorknob and looked back at her.

There was a speculative gleam in his eyes, and Delainey felt a little quiver run through her. What was he going to say...or demand?

''Have something hot,'' he said quietly. ''A cup of tea or a bath. It'll make you feel better.''

She was trembling all over now, and it was difficult even to nod. The action felt jerky and awkward. ''Thanks, Sam.''

''Any time,'' he said. ''Just call for Sir Galahad.''

By morning, Delainey had regained her usual calm and had even found some humor in the events of the evening. She was far from dismissing the incident as unimportant, and whatever it took, she would make sure never to be alone with Curtis Whittington. Still, the very idea of Jason and Curtis negotiating over her as if they were swapping geisha girls was ludicrous.

So ludicrous, in fact, that there was no point in reporting it, for she suspected that nobody at the bank would believe such a story of smooth, polished Jason Conners. It would be far easier to believe that Delainey—new to this end of the banking business, unused to entertaining mega-mogul clients—had simply misinterpreted the events, overreacted to a little heavy-handed masculine teasing, jumped to conclusions.

She might have thought that herself, in fact—if she hadn't been there.

She was just putting on her coat when the doorbell rang, and she peeked out cautiously before she pulled the door open.

Sam was on the doorstep, bending to pick up the morning newspaper from where it lay on the welcome mat.

''You're up early this morning,'' Delainey said. ''Let me

guess. You came to borrow a cup of sugar for your cereal. Or maybe you need something to read to keep you entertained today.''

''No, thanks—I already have a book I'm working my way through.'' Sam held out the newspaper. ''Actually, I noticed as I was running that you hadn't picked this up yet.''

Delainey looked from the mat to the street, estimating the distance. ''You have extraordinarily good vision,'' she mused. ''Admit it, you were checking to be sure I didn't hang myself last night in despair over Curtis Whittington making a pass.''

''Are you all right?''

''I'm fine.''

''Good. Want to play squash tonight? There's a court in the basement of the mansion. You can pretend the ball is the merger maniac's face.''

She didn't answer but pointed past him toward the street. ''Isn't that your cat? I thought she was an indoor, lounge-on-a-pillow type.''

''She is not my cat,'' he said. ''And the Empress does whatever she wants. When she's indoors, she requests whoever's handy to make it warm and pleasant so she can go out. Then when she's out, she wants back in—instantly. And she does it all at the top of her lungs. You have no idea how incredibly spoiled this animal is.''

Delainey smothered a smile at the idea of one of Emma's darlings complaining about the other one. ''What's the matter? Do you and the Empress have a little sibling rivalry going, or something?''

''No, it's more like out-and-out war. Let me know about the squash game.''

''Sure, I'd love to get some exercise. I'll call you when I get home.'' She started to close the door and paused, puzzled. ''Sam—how did you know I play squash?''

Sam grinned. ''Because it's a requirement for any woman I plan to marry.''

For an instant, Delainey's insides twisted, and then she relaxed. "Hey, I thought we agreed the joke was over. Anyway, you sound as if there are rafts of them—women you're engaged to, I mean."

"Oh, no. Just a few."

"Well, that's a relief," Delainey murmured. "Because I only join exclusive clubs."

Josie was obviously bursting with questions, but she had been too well-trained to ask. "Dinner was fine," Delainey said briskly as she took off her coat. "The reservation was perfect, the table was just right, the food was good, the ambience was delightful. I'd recommend it to anyone who asks."

Josie gave a big sigh. "I was so afraid I'd mess it up and you'd be unhappy with me. I brought you something, by the way. A housewarming gift." She reached under her desk and held out a square package wrapped in glossy white paper.

"You shouldn't have, Josie."

"It's nothing, just a bird feeder. It's your first house— and a house needs birds."

Delainey was touched. "Thank you. I hadn't even thought of feeding the birds. My apartment didn't have a balcony or anything, so I've never been in the habit."

"There's a bag of seed in there, too, to get you started." Josie pulled the day's schedule out of the printer tray. "You've got an appointment with—"

The door opened and Jason came in. "I see you finally got to work this morning."

Delainey refused to rise to the bait. She'd been on time, and she didn't doubt that Jason knew it as well as she did. "What can I do for you this morning?"

"RJ wants to see us at ten to report on the progress we've made with Curtis Whittington, such as it is. I'd have done better without you last night. Great team spirit you've got, Delainey."

"Next time," Delainey said crisply, "let me know up front what the game plan is, and I'll sit it out on the bench if I don't like the rules."

"All you had to do was be friendly. Instead, your boyfriend pops up and starts making threats."

Delainey saw Josie's eyes go wide.

"What does he do, anyway, this celebrated boyfriend? Oh, sorry—the word you used was fiancé, wasn't it?"

Josie's eyes bugged out. Delainey noted that unfortunately Jason had seen the woman's reaction, too.

"Odd," he mused, "that nobody around here seems to have heard of him before."

Delainey said coolly, "Marital status and plans are not a part of a standard job interview, Jason. And I prefer to keep personal information personal—that's all."

"What's wrong with him, Delainey?"

"Oh, I'm sure you'd find lots of things to complain about. A great many more than I have time to discuss this morning if I'm going to meet with RJ at ten."

"Just don't dish up your fantasies about what happened last night to RJ."

Delainey had no intention of doing so—but why tell Jason that and put him at ease? Let the jerk sweat a little. "Why shouldn't I? Are you afraid he'll believe me?"

Jason muttered something under his breath and left the room.

"A fiancé? You're engaged?" Josie was breathless and her face was glowing. "That's great!"

"Um—" Delainey took a second look at the secretary. *Now what?*

She could confirm the story and count on Josie's enthusiasm to spread the word and convince the entire office—but that would be a lie. Or she could deny it, confide in Josie about what had happened…and if a hint of the truth leaked to Jason, she'd be toast.

Talk about your basic ethical dilemma.

"We'll have a bridal shower for you," Josie said. "I

know all the girls will be as excited as I am—they all like you, Delainey. Most of them are jealous of me, getting to work with you. When's the wedding?''

"There's no date set," Delainey said. *It's the truth—as far as it goes. Of course, it doesn't get me off the hook entirely.* "But I couldn't allow a shower—RJ would have a fit."

"Oh, we wouldn't have it here," Josie said. "Maybe at a restaurant… What's his name? What does he do?''

He's been laid off. That would go over great. She grabbed at a straw. There was something Sam had said this morning…yes, that was it. "He's working on a book.''

"An author? That's fantastic!''

Delainey heard a sudden bustle in the corridor outside her office. Pounding feet and raised voices were unusual in the sedate halls of the business loan division.

The door flew open and a receptionist burst in. "Josie, have you heard?'' The woman saw Delainey and paused, consternation on her face.

A new piece of hot gossip, Delainey deduced. *Quite possibly about me.*

"Don't mind my being here," Delainey said wryly. "Go right ahead.''

"It's just…'' the receptionist said. "It's RJ. I'm sorry— Mr. Bishop, I mean. He collapsed in the break room a few minutes ago. They think he's had a heart attack.''

Delainey's first thought was concern for the old man. Her second—though she was ashamed of herself for even considering it at a time like this—was for herself.

Because, even under the best of circumstances, RJ was going to be out of the office for a while. And his absence left Jason Conners squarely in charge.

CHAPTER FOUR

BY FOUR o'clock that afternoon, RJ was holding his own in cardiac intensive care, and Jason had relocated to the old man's desk. He made it a point to tell the staff that he'd moved only because RJ's was the one office large enough to accommodate everyone who worked in the department for a briefing on the boss's condition.

But as she listened to the update, Delainey noted that RJ's pen tray and golf trophy had been moved from the desk to a shelf across the room, and a new-looking gold-plated desk set and an Art Deco picture frame had appeared instead.

When the meeting was over and the staff was leaving the room, Jason called Delainey's name. "Stay a minute," he said. "We need to sort out a few things."

Delainey sat down across from the desk. Jason didn't move from the commanding position he'd taken, perched on one corner. As the door closed behind the last secretary, he said, "RJ's absence not only means that the loans he was working on will need to be kept up to date, but all of our clients will need to be reassured about the continuity of services."

Delainey remained silent.

"I've made a list. Here are the loans you will be responsible for pursuing."

She glanced at the paper he handed her. "I had no idea RJ was working on so many deals."

"I gave you most of them. I kept a few—"

No doubt the biggest and most prestigious ones. "What about the other loan officers?" she asked dryly. "Won't they feel left out?"

"They have their own portfolios to handle. Since you're new, you haven't built yours up yet. I'd help out more, but I'll have my hands full with public relations. I'll be contacting every client to assure them that RJ's illness will not affect their business dealings."

Too bad it isn't golf season, Delainey thought. *Then you could really enjoy being on public relations duty.*

Jason shifted on the corner of the desk as if he was ready to stand. "RJ's secretary is pulling all the files for you. I'll expect a report on the status of each case by tomorrow morning."

"You'll have it."

"Sorry if that keeps you from enjoying the boyfriend tonight," Jason sneered. "But he might as well get used to it. You're going to be very busy from now on."

With every nuisance, oddball, time-consuming, and brainless job you can think of. I get the picture.

"If the secretaries got it right," Jason went on, "he's a budding author. Is that a fact?"

Delainey realized she'd been dead on target with her assessment of how little time it would take news to spread through the office once Josie was in possession of it. Of course, being correct wasn't much consolation at the moment.

Fortunately, Jason didn't wait for an answer. "That must mean he's pretty busy himself. Unless he's one of those dabblers in the art of fiction who take an entire lifetime to write a book while allowing someone else the honor of supporting their habit."

"He's quite self-sufficient, thanks." Delainey stood up. "I'll get to work."

She was at the door when Jason spoke. "If there's anything else I need from you, Delainey, I'll let you know."

Delainey didn't doubt it a bit.

Josie had taken one look at the stack of folders Delainey had brought from RJ's office and gone to borrow a couple of tote bags. But it still took two trips for Delainey to get it all into the town house. Since the biggest flat surface in the entire house was the kitchen snack bar, she set the bags on the floor and began to sort the folders into neat piles.

Some of the applications she already had a nodding familiarity with, just through casual discussion with RJ. Other clients she'd never heard of before, and those would require some serious study.

"I thought I was finished with all-nighters when I finally got my degree," she grumbled. She started the coffeepot and picked up the phone to call Sam to cancel their squash game. But she decided instead to walk over and tell him in person. That way she could take advantage of the last bit of sunlight she was apt to see today. And perhaps the fresh air would blow away her headache. It had been nagging at her since she'd had her little chat with Jason, but practically standing on her head to unpack the folders had made it worse.

Emma came to the door. "Sam's not home yet," she said cheerfully. "I sent him to drop off the dry cleaning. I've been planning your housewarming party, dear. Is there anyone at the bank you'd like me to invite?"

The reminder of the party brought Delainey up short. The very idea of a housewarming reminded her of the mortgage she'd signed—a debt that today had grown in her mind to mammoth proportions. If her job was in danger—as it clearly was with Jason in charge of the office—was she going to be able to make the payments?

"Your boss?" Emma added helpfully. "Your secretary?"

"I'll have to let you know," Delainey said.

As she turned away from the door, a bird—some sort of woodpecker, she thought—landed on the bare branch of the tree in Emma's front lawn and sat looking inquisitively at her, head turned to one side.

That reminded Delainey of the bird feeder Josie had given her, and in a spirit of rebellion she went to get the package out of her car. She'd hang it up now, so at least she could look up from her work now and then, see the birds outside, and think about being as free as they were from the cares of the business world.

She was trying to insert the hanging hook into a support next to the front door when she heard the muted roar of a motorcycle coming up the street. She thought it amazing that White Oaks allowed anything so noisy on the premises. Though since Sam didn't seem to pay much attention to other rules, maybe he was simply ignoring that one as well.

The motorcycle pulled into Emma's driveway and the engine died. "Want a hand?" Sam called.

"I'm doing fine."

He came across the lawn anyway. "Have you heard of coats? They're to keep you warm when you work outside."

Delainey pulled her sweater a little closer. "I was just running over to tell you I have to cancel our game, and I decided to stop and do this while I was out."

He took the feeder out of her hands and in two minutes had finished what she'd been struggling with for fifteen. "In the house," he ordered, and followed her. "Now what's this about our game?"

"Too much work to do." Delainey waved a hand toward the snack bar.

"I'd say. It looks to me as if you should have invested part of your furniture budget in a table this month instead of putting every cent of it into a bed." Sam set the helmet atop a stack of files and perched on a bar stool. "What's going on?"

She poured him a cup of coffee as she told him about RJ's illness, and about Jason's move into the main office.

"So the jerk just promoted himself?" Sam asked thoughtfully.

"He's officially been the second in command, so he was

only following procedure when he stepped into RJ's shoes. The problem is, now he's in a position to give me orders—and at the moment, there's no guessing how long that state of affairs will go on. Weeks at least, till RJ's back in the office.''

"And he's taking advantage of every minute in the meantime. I've worked for people like that.''

"Good.'' Delainey watched his eyebrows arch and added hastily, ''No, I don't mean I'm glad you had the same problem. I just thought maybe you can give me some suggestions about how to deal with it.''

Sam shrugged. "I don't know if my experience will help you any. I handled it by quitting.''

"Unfortunately, I can't do that. I can start looking for a job—and I'd better, because if RJ doesn't come back, Jason will be prospecting for reasons to fire me. But I can't just quit right now. Not with a mortgage and all.'' She looked past the snack bar at the rest of the living area—still almost empty except for her futon, now substituting for a couch in front of the empty fireplace—and came to a decision. ''I need to get the town house ready to sell.''

Just saying the words felt like she was admitting defeat, and it tasted brassy on her tongue. It felt as if she was saying she'd been knocked down so hard that she wasn't going to be able to get back on her feet. The very idea of giving up the town house—the symbol of everything she'd worked so hard for—made her ache.

But she had to face the twin realities that her paycheck was at risk and that she had no one to count on but herself. Without an income, she couldn't possibly afford the mortgage. And if that was what was going to happen, the sooner she admitted it and made changes to compensate, the less the long-term damage would be.

Sam's eyebrows rose sharply. "But you just bought it.''

"Don't rub it in, all right?''

"The budget's that tight?'' He sounded neither condemning nor sympathetic, but as if he knew exactly how it felt.

Delainey was grateful for the matter-of-fact approach. "Not at the moment, no. And I could absorb a cut in pay if I had to—if it wasn't too much—and still afford to live here. I wasn't completely foolish about how much debt I took on."

"But it would be much harder to make ends meet."

She nodded. "And if my next job is in another city, I won't be able to keep the town house, so I may as well face the possibility right now. I make good money, but there aren't a lot of jobs like this one."

"I've got the answer. You loan me a few million, we'll split the commission, and—"

"Commission? That's not quite the way it works in the banking industry—my bonus plan is not based on loan volume. Anyway, all of that is beside the point. If the town house is ready to go on the market, I'll be just a little ahead of the game—if it comes down to that. And if it doesn't—well, I'll have the work done that needs doing anyway."

"Rotten timing, buying it when you did. You probably haven't even made a single payment."

He was right, of course. "No doubt it would have been more sensible to wait till I'd been in the job for a while," Delainey admitted. "But I've been at the bank for ten years. It's not like I made a leap with my eyes closed. And it seemed the right thing to do—my roommate was getting married, and I didn't like the apartment all that much. So rather than keep it by myself or look for a new roommate, I decided to make the big change."

"I don't suppose there's ever a perfect time to do something like that."

"No." She sighed. "Because no matter how stable your life seems on any particular day, one little thing—an accident, a new boss, some wacky decision made by a suit three levels up in the corporation—and everything's suddenly turned upside down and you can't do a thing about it.''

''Yeah,'' Sam said wryly. ''I've had some experiences along those lines.''

And that explains why you're living with your grand- mother, Delainey mused. But the fact that he knew exactly what she was talking about gave her an idea. With any luck, it might be an answer and a bonus for both of them....

''To sell the town house,'' she said briskly, ''I first have to get it into better shape.''

''Why? You bought it this way. Why wouldn't someone else?''

''I bought it at a very deep discount because Patty—my real estate broker—told me it had been on the market un- usually long for White Oaks. If I do have to sell, I can't afford to wait. I'll need a quick turnover, and it wouldn't hurt my feelings any to make a profit, either.''

''Profit's a good thing,'' Sam acknowledged.

''Will you help me?''

He darted a glance over his shoulder as if he were hoping she might be talking to someone else, someone who just happened to be standing behind him. ''You're asking me?''

''You've got some handyman skills. I'm sure you can do the things it needs—like painting the walls and fixing the countertop where it's scorched.'' She pointed. ''There's a couple of cracked tile in the bathroom, too, and some perfectly awful scratches in the woodwork upstairs. Can you lay carpet?''

''I don't do carpet—and don't take that to mean I've agreed to tackle the other things, because I haven't. Why me, anyway?''

''Because I can't afford a contractor, and I also don't have time to wait for one to get around to doing my job. Just getting on somebody's list could take months.''

''But you *can* afford me? Honey—''

She was exasperated. ''I'm not asking you to do it for

free, Sam. I just can't afford to pay out a lot of money up front.''

"I still don't see why you think I should be interested in this project.''

"You do the work, and I'll split the profits with you.''

He looked thoughtful. "Down the middle?''

"You drive a mean bargain. All right. Whatever the town house brings—above the price I paid, of course, and after the cost of materials—you get half. All you're investing is your time, and you have plenty of that right now.''

"Ouch.''

"You asked for it. If you do a really good job, it'll sell for a higher price, and you'll make more. Plus I'll give you a reference for your business.''

"Are you still going on about that odd-job business you want to set me up in?''

"Sam, it's a terrific idea. Look, this way, you can try it out without even buying business cards. If you like doing the work—''

"Care to place any bets on the possibility?''

"Of course not. You'd be determined to hate it if the alternative was to pay up. Anyway, if you like it, you'll have some seed money to get you started, and you might not even need that loan we talked about.''

"And a darn good thing, too, if you're likely to be out of the banking business by then. Do you always take such a rosy view of your customers' business prospects, or are you enthusiastic only because you stand to benefit so much from this particular deal? Never mind. Personally, I think you have a lot bigger problems right now than the town house.''

Delainey frowned. "Such as…?''

"You're worried about Jason finding a reason to fire you. Maybe it hasn't dawned on you, but you've already given him one.''

"I don't understand what you mean.''

"That's what I thought. Last night when you introduced me as your fiancé, you thought you were just playing a prank on a co-worker."

"And on you," she admitted. "I know it was a silly thing to do, but—"

"It's a lot worse than silly. It was the world's worst timing. Now he's suddenly become your boss, and he knows you lied to him last night—or at least, he suspects it."

"That's putting it pretty strongly, Sam. You're making it sound like I was—"

"The question is, how is Jason going to make it sound?"

Under the circumstances, Delainey admitted, Jason would put the worst possible construction on what she'd said.

"Lying to the boss," Sam went on, "is a lot different from pulling a prank on a co-worker. All he has to do is prove it, and he can fire you in a minute."

Delainey bit her lip, hard.

"Even your real boss wouldn't make too much of a fuss if he comes back to find you gone under those circumstances," Sam mused. "At least, I don't imagine lying— no matter what it's about—is a good item on a banker's résumé."

Delainey shook her head. "No, it's not—you're right."

"I suppose if you told him right away that it was just a trick—"

But she couldn't, Delainey realized. It would have been bad enough if she'd just stayed silent today when Jason had asked about her supposed fiancé. Even that would have been lying by omission, she supposed—or at least Jason would take it that way. But she hadn't stopped there. She'd told that tall tale about the book, too...

Sam seemed to see the answer in her eyes, for he sighed. "That's what I was afraid of. You don't need a contractor right now, Delainey, you need a fiancé."

"Yeah, the same way I need an infected tooth," Delainey muttered. She felt like banging her head against the wall, except the only thing that would accomplish would be to leave dents which would have to be fixed. What had she been thinking last night, when she'd made that incredibly stupid announcement? And then when she'd expanded on it today?

You should have expected that trying to teach Sam Wagner a lesson would backfire.

But it was too late now—she'd stuck her foot in her mouth, and she'd simply have to deal with the fallout. "You've got a point there," she admitted.

"So you can either confess to Jason that you've been leading him on—"

"Which would give him exactly the ammunition he needs to fire me."

"Or you can keep right on lying—and make it look very convincing."

Put that way, there wasn't much choice. "So does that mean you're volunteering to keep posing as…as my fiancé?" The word felt funny on her tongue, now that it suddenly wasn't quite so much of a joke.

"What's it worth to you?"

"Dammit, Sam—you know I'm in a bind here. You got me into this, so you have to help me out."

His eyes widened. "What do you mean, *I* got you into this?"

"You certainly did—you butted in and so I had to explain you. Never mind, that doesn't matter now. The fact is I can't go hire an actor—it's *you* I have to have."

He grinned. "Darling, just to hear you say how much you need me is such a turn-on I can hardly bear it."

Delainey glared at him. "Fine. I *don't* need you—I'll just announce that the engagement's broken, and—"

"And you think Jason will believe that convenient coincidence? You might as well confess as tell him a fairy tale of that magnitude.''

The trouble was, Delainey thought, he was probably right.

"So I'll ask again,'' Sam said. "What's it worth to you?''

"I'll tell you what it's *not* worth. I'm not going to bed with you.''

"I didn't suggest it,'' Sam said coolly. "And I won't even ask what makes you think that would be adequate payment.''

Delainey's jaw dropped. "You arrogant—''

"Wait just a minute here—who are you calling arrogant? Anyway, the question of payment will depend on how long this performance goes on—among other things.''

"Under the best of circumstances, RJ won't be back in the office full-time for a few weeks.'' She swallowed hard. "If he doesn't make it…'' The thought was almost too much to bear. "If he doesn't come back at all, and Jason's named the new director, I'll be job-hunting furiously. A month. Perhaps more.''

"That could have its complications,'' Sam mused. "A month's a pretty long time. How long till you know for sure whether he'll be coming back?''

"A couple of weeks, maybe. How about if we agree to make it look good for that long? Then we stage a tremendous fight, break the engagement, and we're finished.''

"A couple of weeks,'' he said thoughtfully.

Delainey was exasperated. "It's not like every minute of your day's committed, Sam.''

"Hey, I have things to do. Play squash, wash Gran's car, watch golf tournaments—''

"How much effort can it take to play this part? You drop into the bank a time or two—that's it.''

"All right,'' he said finally. "I'll do it. And I'll figure out later what you can do for me in return.''

It was like signing a blank check. The very idea left Delainey feeling a little hollow—but she didn't have many options at the moment. She either accepted Sam's vaguely threatening terms, or she confessed to Jason—and if she did that, she'd be out of a job by tomorrow morning.

Of course—with any luck—by the time Sam made up his mind what he wanted, she wouldn't need him anymore, and she might not have to pay up after all.

That would be a dirty trick, her conscience whispered. But then, Sam couldn't exactly claim the moral high ground either, when he was forcing her to bargain in the dark.

"I guess if that's my choice, I'll take it," she said.

"Grudging, but it'll have to do." Sam looked her straight in the eye. "Hi. I'm your new and improved fiancé."

"Uh—yeah."

He frowned a little. "I get the feeling there should be some ceremony here, considering the importance of the occasion."

Something like a kiss, I suppose? Don't be ridiculous.

Sam's face cleared, and he grabbed her hand and pumped vigorously. "There. It's officially a deal. Let's go play squash."

Delainey shook her head. "Remember? I've got too much work to do."

"You'll do it better after you've smashed a ball around for a while to get your frustration level down."

There was some truth to that—especially if the alternative was having him hang around the town house distracting her. But at least he hadn't insisted on sealing the deal with a kiss....

"All right, I'll go change. Oh, by the way," she called from the stairs. "Just so I don't forget to tell you—everybody at my office thinks you're writing a book."

"By the time this adventure is over," Sam said, not quite under his breath, "I'll probably be able to."

* * *

Sam was right about the squash game. He was a fiendish opponent and Delainey was drenched, breathless, and limp by the time she got home. The trouble was, she was more ready for a nap than for work, but she couldn't avoid the stacks of folders or the knowledge that Jason would be quizzing her about them in the morning. So she made a fresh pot of strong coffee and settled down at the breakfast bar.

But she couldn't shake the feeling that somewhere she'd overlooked something major, and the sensation continued to nag at her while she dug through the first dozen of RJ's pending loans. What was it she was forgetting? Something about work? About Jason? About Sam?

She pretended not to hear the phone when it rang—the last thing she needed was to be interrupted by a telemarketer—but the fist banging on the patio door a few minutes later couldn't be ignored. Sam was outside, carrying a shopping bag emblazoned with the Tyler-Royale department store logo.

"An engagement present?" Delainey said. "For me? Oh, how thrilling. I'm so sorry I forgot to get you something, but then it is traditional for the man to be the one who—"

"It's your dinner. Gran figured if you were working so hard, you'd forget to eat."

Delainey wasn't listening. "Engagement present! Of course, that's what's been bothering me. I'd forgotten all about... Now where did I put it?"

She started digging through kitchen drawers. She knew the item she was looking for had been in one of the two boxes of special treasures that she'd moved to the town house herself and unpacked the first night. She remembered taking the blue-velvet case out of the box. But what had she done with it then? Had it been before or after the fire fiasco that she'd unpacked it? Had she taken it upstairs, or shoved it into a convenient corner in the kitchen?

"Where did you put what?" Sam asked. He set the shopping bag on the counter and took out a stack of plastic containers.

"My mother's diamond ring. Here it is." With a sigh of relief, Delainey extracted the worn blue-velvet case from between her silver sugar tongs and a set of plastic chopsticks and opened it.

Sam was looking over her shoulder. "That's a diamond ring? Where's the diamond?"

Delainey would have stuck her tongue out at him, except that she was having much the same reaction herself. How could a ring look so different in real life than in her memories?

It was without a doubt the same ring she remembered from her childhood, when she'd often begged—and occasionally been granted—the privilege of trying it on. In the eyes of a child, it had been wonderfully, romantically sparkly—a real diamond ring, fit for a princess to wear. Now the band looked old, dull, and worn, and the stone was so small it was practically invisible.

"It needs cleaning." She was trying as much to persuade herself as to convince him. "It'll brighten up."

"I'm being very careful here not to say anything about your mother's taste or your father's budget," Sam said, "but if you think that's going to convince Jason, you're even more of an optimist than I thought."

"It's the sentimental value that's important," Delainey explained. "It's not only an antique, it's been in the family forever."

Sam rolled his eyes.

Delainey tried again. "Besides, you're a writer, remember? So you don't have money for elaborate rings."

But the words felt hollow. It wasn't only Jason who'd have to be convinced, she reminded herself. Every woman in the office would take one look at that ring and start whispering behind Delainey's back—and their opinions would get back to Jason within minutes.

"Right," Sam said. Doubt dripped from his voice.

Delainey's temper flared. "Look, I don't know what else to do. I can't afford to go buy something that would be really impressive. Maybe Emma has something I could borrow. It doesn't even have to be a ring, just something I could say was an engagement gift."

"Gran's not big on lending things like real diamonds," Sam said.

"Of course." Delainey felt herself flush. "I'm sorry. That was a really stupid thing to ask. Does she even know about this stunt yet?"

"Yeah, I told her. Where do you keep the plates?"

Delainey pointed to the cabinet, waited a minute for him to answer, and finally asked tentatively, "And what did she think?"

"That's when she started cooking up a storm." He began spooning pasta and tomato sauce onto the plates.

Delainey took a deep breath. The food smelled divine. "She started cooking?"

"Yeah. It's apparently one of those women things—the mere mention of a wedding or a baby and they start in with all kinds of craziness."

"Nesting instincts," Delainey said absently. "But you told her it's not real—right?"

"Of course. That's what I don't understand about this— what did you call it? Nesting? I'd rather have stomach cramps, myself. Here." He reached into his pocket and held out his hand.

On his palm sparkled a ring, a gold-colored band holding a single round, yellowish stone that flashed in the light.

Delainey stared at it, and then at him. "Please tell me you didn't raid Emma's jewelry box while she was busy in the kitchen."

"No, I didn't heist the ring off Gran's dressing table. I

bought it, if that makes you feel better.'' He held it up to the light. ''Wonderful things they're doing with cubic zirconia these days.''

Delainey took the ring out of his hand and looked at it closely, and then she released the breath she'd been holding. ''It's amazing, isn't it? It wouldn't pass a close inspection, of course—it doesn't have quite the same fire as a real stone and it's a little too showy somehow. But at a glance…'' She slipped the ring on and turned her hand in the light. ''It's just a little loose, but I don't suppose it can be resized.''

''Not a good idea,'' Sam said.

''Thanks for thinking of it, Sam. Put it on your list and I'll reimburse you.''

''The list of things I'm supposed to buy to fix up the town house? Paint and stuff like that?''

''That's the one.''

''I was meaning to talk to you about that.''

She noted that he was dishing up a second plate. ''Gee, I hope you'll be able to stay for dinner, Sam.''

''Gran was afraid that even with food right under your nose you might forget to eat unless someone was reminding you.''

''I see. So she assigned you the duty of making me eat.''

''I get stuck with all the jobs she doesn't want,'' Sam said earnestly. ''And just look at where I end up because of it.''

Delainey handed him a fork, shoved a stack of folders aside, and sat down with her plate. ''You're absolutely certain she understands this isn't a real engagement?''

''Gran's a romantic, Delainey, but she's not an idiot.''

''Well, that's reassuring. I mean, we've only known each other for three days, so to think that we could have formed any kind of serious bond here…'' She savored a bite of manicotti and sighed. ''On the other hand, if marrying you would mean Emma would cook for me regularly, I might give the whole idea more thought.''

"Don't threaten me like that." He pulled up a bar stool next to her and pointed his fork at the stack of folders she'd pushed aside. "What is it you have to do with all of these?''

"Pop quiz tomorrow," she said lightly.

"Is this like working out word problems in math? Those are always fun. 'If Robert Jones wants to borrow two hundred and seventy-five thousand dollars at six percent, how soon will the payments drive him into bankruptcy?' I could grill you.''

"Those are confidential files, Sam. Hands off.''

"You keep secrets from your fiancé?'' Sam sounded almost hurt.

Delainey wasn't listening. "I had such high hopes for this job," she mused. "I think I could have even convinced RJ to fund my incubator idea.''

"Uh—Delainey, what are you trying to incubate?''

"Women's businesses. Small ones, mostly—helping them to get off the ground.''

"That's a relief—I thought you might be talking about eggs. So if, say, Emma was wanting to start making scarves and mittens to sell…''

"I could get her a loan for a knitting machine. And she could set it up in a room in a little office complex where there would be one receptionist to answer the phones and take orders for everybody, and a shared copy machine she could use for patterns and bills, and—''

"A knitting machine? She'd sniff and say, 'Where's the fun in that?'''

"No doubt. Seriously, though, women still don't have as many opportunities in the business world as men do. Partly it's because their ideas are often smaller.''

"Careful—there are women who would string you up for saying things like that.''

"It's true, though. Many women focus their businesses at least initially on feminine ideas and feminine markets. Jewelry, candles, crafts, body lotions, home decorations. And because they're very small businesses, run by women and targeted at women, many men in the financial community don't have the imagination to take them seriously."

"You were going to change that."

"I was going to try," Delainey said softly.

"Well, don't give it up just yet."

She was touched. "That's sweet, Sam. You having faith in me."

"I hate to break your heart," Sam said cheerfully, "but it's got nothing to do with faith. I'm hoping you'll find a woman somewhere who's got a few do-it-yourself skills and wants to be set up in the handyman business—so you'll leave me out of it."

CHAPTER FIVE

WHEN Delainey walked into the bank the next morning lugging the heavy tote bags, she expected that it wouldn't take Josie long to spot the ring on her left hand. What surprised her was that the actual elapsed time was something short of half a second and that Josie's eyes not only bugged out but the secretary leaped up so fast that her chair went spinning across to bang into the credenza behind her desk.

Delainey had to admit the woman had reason. Sam's ring was the eye-catching variety. A cubic zirconia half that size would have been plenty large enough to make the point.

It was odd, she thought, that Sam's ring could be so much less valuable than the muted little band and diamond chip that her mother had worn for all those years—and yet be so much more ostentatious.

Josie rushed across the room. "Here, let me help you with those files." But she wasn't looking at the tote bags. She was eyeing the ring.

Delainey very deliberately held out the bag in her left hand. *Let Josie take a good look and get it over with.*

The secretary stared and blinked and sighed. "I thought...well, never mind."

Delainey opted to tackle the subject head on. "You thought I wasn't wearing a ring because Sam couldn't afford one."

"Sam—that's his name? You never said yesterday."

"Didn't I?"

"I like it," Josie said. "Sam. It's such a nice solid name." She hadn't taken her eyes off the ring.

Delainey could almost hear the question the secretary

was thinking, so she answered it. "I haven't been wearing it at work because I think a person's wedding plans are a private matter."

Maybe, if she was lucky, that announcement would help to reduce the inevitable curiosity—or at least keep it far enough underground that she wouldn't face questions every time she set foot in the coffee room.

"It must have been hard to keep such exciting news secret, though."

Not at all—since I didn't know it myself. "I didn't want to cause comment. But of course now that everybody knows, it seemed silly to leave the ring at home."

"Seeing that will cause comment, all right." Josie shot a sideways glance at Delainey and reached for the second tote bag. "What do you want me to do with all these? Take them back to RJ's secretary?"

"No, hang on to them for the moment. Some can wait till RJ's back, but others will need action much sooner than that. It would be very helpful if you could sort them by date."

Josie nodded. "So that the ones which require your attention first are on top of the stack? I can do that right away."

Delainey hung up her coat and went on into her office. But her mind wasn't totally on business. She was still thinking about that shrewd look of Josie's and her almost-cryptic comment.

It'll cause comment, all right.

And exactly what had she meant by that? Had Josie recognized the ring for the fraud it really was?

Delainey wouldn't have expected her secretary to be an amateur jeweler. On the other hand, a stone that size simply begged to be inspected. It was dead certain that no woman could come anywhere within ten feet of it and not take a close second look. And if a woman had experience with things like diamond rings...

She sat down at her desk and held up her left hand, fingers spread, to study the ring. In the light from her desk lamp, the stone looked more yellow than it had last night in her kitchen. A yellow tone wasn't a good thing in diamonds, as she recalled. Had that fact given the game away to Josie?

"I guess I'll find out soon enough," Delainey muttered. If Josie wasn't convinced, the entire staff would be buzzing by the morning coffee break, and by lunchtime half of them would have found excuses to come in and talk to her and take a look for themselves.

Whatever happened, it was clearly too late to do anything about it. Still, she couldn't help wishing that Sam had shown just a little more restraint when he'd visited the jewelry counter of the five-and-dime.

Delainey stabbed a chunk of roasted chicken from atop her salad and looked across the table at a blond woman who wore the dark green jacket of a national chain of real estate agents.

"So that's the way things stand, Patty," she said. "It looks like I might be putting the town house up for sale before I ever make a payment."

The blonde stopped toying with her egg-white omelette and reached for her electronic calendar. "You don't need to apologize to me for changing your mind. That's how I make my living."

"And a good living it is, the way this is shaping up," Delainey said dryly. "I mean really, Patty, when you're selling it for the second time in just a couple of months—"

"You think I should give you a reduced rate?" Patty smiled and shook her head. "Nope. I should charge you extra, because I'll have to explain to the next buyer why you lasted less than a month there, and that isn't going to be easy. The place isn't haunted, is it?"

Just by the neighbor. "The only bumps in the night I've

heard have been when I walked into a door.'' She eyed the blonde over the rim of her iced-tea glass. ''What are you doing, Patty?''

Patty looked up from the minuscule screen of the calendar. ''Making myself a note to do the paperwork for the listing.''

''Wait a minute. I'm not ready to actually put it up for sale yet. I was just saying that I'll probably—''

Patty shrugged. ''I believe in being prepared—when you're ready to sign, the papers will be waiting. By the way, do you want to tell me about that?'' She pointed at Delainey's left hand.

''Oh.'' Delainey looked down at the ring. ''I guess I'd forgotten about it.''

Patty shook her head. ''Try a different sort of fable, my friend, because I'm not buying that one. It must be like lifting a weight every time you raise your hand.''

Delainey took a big bite of lettuce just so she could have a chance to think.

''I'm surprised, you know.'' Patty put the calendar away and broke a bread stick in half with a snap.

''That I'm…engaged?'' Delainey was still having trouble with the word because whenever she tried to say it, she felt as if her tongue had gone all fuzzy.

''Not the getting-married part, just the ring. It doesn't seem like you somehow.''

''Really?'' Delainey held out her hand and looked at the ring once more. In the muted light of the restaurant, the stone didn't glare and it didn't look so yellow. Even the mounting looked more restrained, so she was curious about Patty's reaction. ''Why don't you think it's my style?''

''I'd have expected you to choose a smaller stone, but one that was absolutely perfect. And a simpler setting instead of something quite so…''

''Garish?''

''Well…that wasn't the word I'd have chosen, but—''

"Sam picked it out."

"I see," Patty said dryly. "Well, if you take my advice you'll train him right from the beginning, or you'll never in your life get a single Christmas gift that you won't have to exchange. His name's Sam? I've never heard you mention a Sam."

That's because I haven't seen you since I met him. "I wanted to wait to talk about him till I was sure."

Patty's eyebrows rose a fraction, but to Delainey's relief she changed the subject. "I found you a building that would be great for your business incubator."

"I'm afraid that whole project is on hold for now." Delainey sighed. "No, the truth is it's not even far along to be put on hold. I was only starting to work on RJ about the possibilities when he got sick. And the man who's in charge now..."

"Say no more. What you're telling me is that the whole idea's on life support."

"And not showing much in the way of brain waves."

"That's too bad. It was a great idea—even if I'm not the one who collects the commission for selling the building." She pointed at Delainey's bag. "Isn't that your pager beeping?"

Delainey blinked in surprise and then dug for the pager. "I'm not quite used to listening for it yet." The pager displayed the number of her own office, but that was no surprise; Delainey had expected that it would be Josie who was calling. But why? If Jason was on the rampage...

Don't jump to conclusions, she told herself. Maybe Josie was just having trouble with some of RJ's loan files. She'd had a problem herself last night, trying to read his handwriting. Of course, it hadn't helped that it had been two o'clock in the morning and she'd started dozing off on almost every page...

Delainey pushed the rest of her salad away. "I think I'd better head back. Sorry to desert you."

"Call me when you're ready to sign the papers." Patty's voice was matter-of-fact, as if selling the town house was no big deal.

And of course, Delainey thought morosely, for Patty it wasn't anything special. "Sure," she said. "I'll see you then."

She paid her bill and walked back to the bank. She wasn't surprised that Josie was spending her lunch hour at her desk, because she usually did. But she was startled to see that the secretary wasn't eating her usual sandwich, and she was even more surprised to see a man sitting in the small waiting area next to Josie's desk. Automatically she assessed him. Well-dressed, probably in his fifties—a salesman of some sort, perhaps.

"Ms. Hodges," Josie said as the man stood up, "Mr. Laurent has been waiting for you. That's why I buzzed." She tapped one of RJ's folders on the desk blotter to settle all the pages in order and then set it atop an unsteady pile on the credenza behind her desk.

"I'm sorry to drag you away from your lunch," the man said. "I don't have an appointment, and Mr. Conners warned me that you might be out."

And the toss-up question, Delainey told herself, was whether Jason had sent a client down on her lunch hour so he could rake her over the coals later for making the man wait, or if he been simply trying to discourage the customer by making him cool his heels for a while.

She opened the door of her office. "Come in, Mr. Laurent. What can I do for you?"

He waited until the door was closed and Delainey was seated behind her desk. "I find myself in need of a short-term loan to tide me over. My business, that is."

She reached for a notepad. "What's your business?"

"I supply packaging materials—everything from generic corrugated cartons to very specialized containers for delicate electronics." He handed her a business card in the flat cutout shape of a tiny box waiting to be folded for use. If she was dexterous enough to put it together, which Delainey doubted she was, the minuscule box might be big enough to hold a penny. "That's a wide range of products."

"Not quite as wide as it sounds. We don't take on a lot of clients, but we work very closely with those we serve. We figure out the cleanest, safest and least expensive way to pack and ship everything our clients make."

"So the client just worries about making the best product, and they don't have to fuss about what kind of a box to put it in."

"Exactly, because we've already thought of it, designed it, and put it together—so everything is there at the end of the production line waiting. They don't have to deal with getting bottles from one supplier and cartons from another, and then making sure that one fits inside the other just right, because we do it all."

"I think I've got the picture. What has caused your cash-flow problem?"

"Our largest customer is—was—Foursquare Electronics."

Delainey nodded. "That's the one which was recently merged into Curtis Whittington's corporation, right?"

Laurent sniffed. "Call it a corporation if you want. Personally I think Whittington's outfit bears more resemblance to the Mafia than to a business."

Judging by her experience with Curtis Whittington himself, Delainey was inclined to agree—though she knew it wouldn't be wise to say so. She settled for making a noncommittal noise.

"Sorry if that sounds like sour grapes," Laurent muttered.

"No, it sounds as if you have a strong opinion, and probably a good reason for it. Care to tell me about it? Why isn't Foursquare a client anymore?"

"We've been working under an arrangement with Foursquare where we deliver packaging and boxes as needed and the company pays the invoice thirty days later."

"That seems fair."

"It's more than fair, because every box has already been used and shipped before it's paid for. We've never had a problem dealing with them on a handshake. But since the takeover, it's a different story. The payments have been coming later with each new billing cycle. When I questioned it, the new management said their policy has changed—now they'll pay in four months instead of one."

Delainey nodded. "Which creates a major cash-flow crisis for you, if you were counting on getting that money sooner."

"Of course I was counting on it. I have to pay my bills, too. And if I don't agree to their payment terms, they'll get their packaging supplies somewhere else from now on."

"Can they do that? Your business sounds unique."

"I'm the best there is—if they care about what they're shipping. But they can slop their product into any old box and send it out. They'll have to write off a bunch of damaged merchandise, of course, but they seem to think that would be cheaper in the long run. And since I expect their next move would be to try to force down my price, I won't be bidding any more jobs for them."

"You could sue for the overdue payment, of course, but—"

"Bringing attorneys in would only tie things up longer. We might be talking years then, instead of a few months' delay."

"Probably true. What about the long run, Mr. Laurent, if you aren't going after their business in the future?"

"I'm developing some clients to fill the gap. But of course it'll take a little time to design and produce their packaging, and then it'll be a while longer before they pay the bill in full. In the meantime—''

"You could use some cash to tide you over." Delainey nodded. "I'll need to look at your books, of course."

"Whatever you want, you've got it. Shall I send my bookkeeper in to talk to you, or would you like to come to the office?"

"I'll come out. Shall we say Monday morning?" She pulled her calendar over. "Nine o'clock?"

"The address is on my card. Ms. Hodges, I can't thank you enough."

Delainey stood up. "I'll do the best I can. But I can't promise the results because I'll have to take the application before our loan committee."

He nodded. "I know you can't guarantee anything, but I feel much better already. More hopeful than I've been since I heard that Foursquare sold out. Not that I blame the owners for taking the offer, because Whittington didn't hesitate to put cash on the barrelhead then. But it made a raw deal for some of us." He shook hands.

"I'll see you Monday morning, Mr. Laurent." Delainey pulled the door open and tried to stifle a gasp as she looked out across Josie's office.

It looked as if a blizzard had struck. The carpet between the secretary's desk and the credenza was invisible, covered with a flood of paper and forms and manila folders that had once been the stack of RJ's loan cases. The collapse must have happened just as Delainey opened the door, because some pages were still drifting, not yet settled on the floor.

Josie was standing in the middle of the mess, hands raised as if to ward off an attack. Horror was etched on her face.

Delainey didn't blame her. The work of an entire morning lay ruined on the carpet. It could take days to get everything back in the right folder.

She walked Mr. Laurent to the lobby and came back,

taking deep breaths all the way in order to maintain her
self-control. Much as she felt like yelling at Josie, there
would be no point in it. It wouldn't fix the damage, and
poor Josie was already going to be paying a terrific penalty
for her carelessness.

Besides, she realized as she came in, Josie wasn't alone.
At the end of the credenza farthest from the door that led
into Delainey's office was a man, kneeling in the midst of
the mess, gathering papers together by the armful, and mut-
tering something about being sorry. Sorry? If he'd caused
the damage, that must mean he'd been there when she'd
ushered Mr. Laurent out. Delainey didn't know how she'd
missed seeing him then, unless he'd been flat on the carpet
and under the credenza.

*If I was the one who'd knocked over Josie's folders, I
wouldn't have stopped at the carpet,* she thought. *I'd have
gone straight on through the floor to the basement rather
than face her.*

She took a second look, sighed, and went to stand over
him, her arms folded across her chest.

"If you're trying to hide from me, Sam," she said, "that
credenza isn't big enough. And if you're on your knees
begging Josie not to kill you for knocking over that stack
of folders, I'm on Josie's side."

Sam rose with dignity, set a double handful of pages on
Josie's blotter and bent to brush off his knees. "As a matter
of fact, when the accident happened, I was doing a demonstration for Josie. I was recreating the elegance of the
way I proposed to you."

"Really? What on earth brought that on?"

"Josie wanted to know all the details."

Josie started to sputter. "Now wait a minute, Mr.
Wagner. If you're blaming *me*—"

"No, no, Josie," Sam said quickly. "I take the full responsibility. Unfortunately, I neglected to restrain my enthusiasm when I came to the part where I offered you the

entire world on a platter—or was it a tray, darling? Do you remember?''

Delainey flipped a mental coin. ''Platter. I remember thinking at the time you were being terribly unoriginal.''

''I must have been swept away by the cliché of the moment. Anyway, I flung out my arms to show the magnitude of my offer and hit the stack of folders, and—'' He shrugged.

''And now you get to help put everything back,'' Josie said.

Delainey shook her head. ''He can't touch those papers.''

''But he's already touched them! That's the whole point!''

''They're confidential.''

Josie's face fell. ''You mean I'm going to have to do it? Can't we hire him and make it all right? Not really hire him, I mean, but go through the motions so he can fix what he did?''

''And pay him a dollar a year,'' Delainey said. ''Which is about how long it'll take to sort out the mess. Sorry, Josie—I can't do it. It's not just the salary—the bank wouldn't like having to pay his benefits. He'll have to make it up to you some other way.'' She jerked a thumb toward her door. ''In my office, Wagner. On the double.''

She shut out the image of Josie's face, woebegone as she contemplated the depth of the disaster outside, and turned to face Sam. ''What brought you here in the first place?''

''You suggested I drop in now and then to make this look good.''

Delainey wasn't listening. ''And what on earth inspired you to recreate the supposed romance of—'' She paused, suddenly suspicious. ''Did you do that on purpose?''

''Make that mess?'' He drew himself up straight. ''Ms. Hodges, that's a terrible thing to accuse a man of. The very idea!''

"You can drop the offended act, Sam."

He grinned. "Okay. What makes you ask such a stupid question, anyway?"

"Because you're not normally clumsy, or you'd have fried yourself a long time ago fixing things like outlets. What I don't see is why you'd have done it." She tapped her index finger against her cheekbone while she thought.

Sam wandered across the room. He appeared to be studying the framed diploma on her wall.

"Oh, now I get it," Delainey said finally. "You wanted to take a look at those folders last night, but I wouldn't let you. So today you tried to arrange it so you could see inside them. If I hadn't popped my head out of my office right then, Josie would have put you to work straightening them out without giving it a second thought, and then you could have seen...whatever it is you're looking for. What is it you want to see, by the way?"

Sam turned around. "You're *good*. Are you absolutely certain I'm the one on this team who's supposed to be deeply into creating fiction?"

"What's in those files that you're dying to see, Sam?"

He flicked a fingertip against the end of her nose. "Nothing, sweetheart."

But the denial didn't quite ring true to Delainey's ears. "You must have caught a glimpse of a name on the tab of one of the folders," she mused. "There's no way you could have seen anything else last night, because I didn't open any of them while you were there. But which name could it have been that got your attention?"

"Whenever you're finished with this flight of fancy, Delainey, I have some paint chips for you to look at."

His sudden shift from playful to matter-of-fact startled her. "Paint chips? What are you talking about?"

"For the town house walls."

"What do I care? Paint it white."

"That much I figured. But—" He pulled a wallet from

the back pocket of his jeans, took out a wad of papers, and began flicking through them with the easy grace of a magician with a deck of cards. "Do you mean off-white? Antique white? Frost white? Grecian white? Dead white European male—no, wait, that's a political statement, not a color. Blush white? Moonlight white? Fog white? White Sands white—I like that one myself. It takes a certain amount of ego for a color to put itself in its name twice."

"Stop it. You're only trying to distract me from the whole thing with the folders. Besides, you said you weren't going to paint. Or fix tiles, or countertops, or—"

"That's why I went to the hardware store to collect all the shades of white," Sam said earnestly. "Because the longer it takes you to decide on one, the less likely it is that I'll ever have to do anything."

"Give me those." She snatched the deck of colors from his hand, fanned them out like a bridge hand, pulled one from the middle, and thrust it at him. "Here. This one."

He looked at it closely. "Okay, if that's what you really want. I bet they'll have to mix it up special, though. There can't be much demand for a shade called Cold Ghostly Specter White."

"Go away, Sam. I have work to do."

"What time will you be home, darling?"

"Not until I've figured out which one of those folders you're interested in."

"You've got folders on the brain, Delainey."

"You could just give me the name."

He shook his head. "No, I can't. I'll tell Gran not to even try to keep your dinner warm, since—knowing you—it'll probably be sometime around the end of next week before you give up."

The expression on Josie's face when Sam came out of Delainey's office, plus the fact that she didn't bother to look up from the folder she was organizing to reply to his goodbye, told him he had some major fence-mending to do there.

He'd have to think hard about that one, he concluded. This faked-up engagement might be scheduled to last only a couple of weeks, but in the meantime life would be much more pleasant if he could stay on the good side of Delainey's secretary. Considering the mess he'd made of her office, however, sweetening Josie up wasn't going to be easy.

Not that he regretted what he'd done. When Delainey's office door had opened and he'd seen the profile of the man standing in the doorway, Sam had had no more than a split second to make a decision. Pulling over that stack of folders had been the only option he could see.

It wasn't that he'd been trying to avoid George Laurent—in fact, he was looking forward to talking to the man. For one thing, he'd really like to know what George had been doing in Delainey's office today. He just didn't particularly want Delainey to be there when he asked.

But, he thought, first things first. Maybe if he bought Josie an entire flower shop's worth of roses, it would make a dent in her armor.

If he was lucky.

Delainey pitched in, and she and Josie had the worst of the mess cleaned up in a couple of hours. It hadn't been quite as bad as it had looked at first. Though every piece of paper still had to be inspected, only a few of the folders had actually exploded.

Josie flicked through the last few pages of an application and said, ''This one looks all right, but you'll need to check it, Ms. Hodges. It's one I hadn't gotten to before the disaster so I don't know what order everything was supposed to be in.''

Delainey cleared off a corner of the credenza so she

could perch on it, and was just immersing herself in the file when Jason Conners looked around the corner.

Though Delainey hadn't given him a thought all afternoon, she supposed she shouldn't be surprised that he'd turned up to take a look. By now, the entire department must know about the tornado that had struck her office.

"The boyfriend made quite a mess, huh? I hope RJ doesn't hear how you've been treating his files."

And how would RJ find out if you don't tell him? Delainey focused on the folder. "Too bad you couldn't drop in earlier when you could still get the full effect."

"I was busy. I'm pulling together a deal for Curtis. How did you get along with George Laurent?"

"Just fine. I'm going out to look at his books on Monday."

"I'd say it's not worth the bother."

"Are you saying the business is too small to trouble ourselves with? Or do you mean you don't want to help somebody get out from under Curtis Whittington's thumb?"

"Under...what are you talking about?"

"That's what's caused his cash-flow problems. Curtis Whittington's takeover and the change in policy to slow pay for the goods they buy."

"And you believed that explanation?"

"Having had a demonstration up close and personal of Mr. Whittington's ethics, I have no reason not to believe George Laurent."

Jason turned brickred. "You've got no cause to talk about Curtis that way."

"Are you saying it was only my imagination when Curtis indicated that if I slept with him he'd do business?"

Jason darted a look at Josie. "I didn't hear him say anything like that—and he's doing business with us, so you'd better not be talking about him. You should be flattered that he's attracted to you—or at least he was."

"Thanks anyway. Jason, the rules might change from time to time, but right and wrong don't." It was senseless to try to discuss it with him, though, she told herself. She'd be wiser to spend the time touching base with her contacts at other banks, seeing if one of them would be interested in giving George Laurent the loan he needed. Because it was quite clear to Delainey that National City wasn't going to, as long as Jason was in charge.

It was almost dark when Delainey gave up on searching RJ's folders for something—anything!—which might have grabbed Sam's attention. When she pulled into her driveway, she saw a cat sitting on her front step, a pale blur in the soft twilight. The Empress was crouched like a statue of a prowling tiger. Her tail was the only thing that twitched, and her big blue eyes were fixed on a cardinal at the feeder.

Delainey got out of the car in the driveway, slamming the door and storming across the handkerchief-size lawn toward the porch. "Go home, you—you stalker! Leave my birds alone!"

The Empress turned her head to look at Delainey, but she was obviously only mildly interested and her attention soon returned to the brilliant red bird.

Delainey tried shooing her away. She even considered picking the animal up and carrying her home, but the Empress seemed to read her mind—she hissed, but she didn't move.

Delainey only vaguely heard the murmur of an engine as a car pulled up to the curb. It was actually the absence of sound that caught her attention the instant the engine died.

She turned around to see who might be coming to visit and wanted to swear. Jason Conners and Curtis Whittington were getting out of the Mercedes.

Make a preemptive strike, she told herself. *Don't even let them ask if they can come in.*

"Hi," she called. "Sorry I can't stop to chat, but you've caught me on my way out." She started to walk toward the driveway. "If you wouldn't mind moving the car a bit so I can back out—"

They didn't pause. Jason pointed at the front windows. "You left the lights on inside the house."

It was news to Delainey. In the few minutes she'd been trying to negotiate with the Empress, twilight had faded into dark—and sure enough, inside the town house the lights were glowing. Had she left them on that morning? She couldn't remember.

"I often do that," she said.

"So you feel safer coming home to an empty house?" Jason suggested. "Or is the boyfriend the one who doesn't like the dark? This will just take a minute. I have some numbers for you to crunch this weekend and I need to show you the figures and explain what I need."

It was a perfectly reasonable request—which was part of the reason Delainey felt so suspicious. She opened her mouth to refuse.

Behind her, the front door of the town house squeaked as it opened. Light from the foyer fell across the porch, silhouetting a tall figure in the opening, and Sam, leaning out, said mildly, "I thought I heard someone out here yelling about a stalker. But I must have been mistaken."

"Stalker?" Jason's voice was higher than usual and almost squeaky. "You can't say things like that!"

Delainey pointed at the Siamese. The cardinal had flown when the two men approached, and the Empress had moved to one side and started bathing herself, looking as innocent as a kitten. "I was talking about your cat, Sam. She's been chasing my birds."

"I told you she's not my cat," Sam said absently. "But I'm glad to know it was only the feline version you were talking about. I'd hate to think you were slandering these fine gentlemen. Hello, Whittington. Conners. Come on in.''

Come in? What on earth was the man thinking?

Delainey tried frantically to catch Sam's eye, but he didn't seem to get the message.

"How brilliant of you, darling," he said gently. "Mr. Whittington will really get a good look at the town house this way."

Was he dense? Didn't he understand that was exactly what she was trying to prevent?

"It's the best way there is to look at a place." Sam looked past her to the two men. "Don't you agree?"

Delainey thought Curtis and Jason looked every bit as wary as she felt.

"I thought you said you were going somewhere, Delainey," Jason said.

Delainey opened her mouth, and closed it again. She didn't want to stay—but she was darned if she was going to leave either. Not with Sam in charge.

"She is," Sam said. "She's going after pizza. It's the least we can do to thank the two of you for volunteering to help us paint."

CHAPTER SIX

SAM stepped back from the door so the visitors could get a better view. The town house was a pretty spectacular sight at the moment, he had to admit. The futon was draped in clear plastic, as was the fireplace mantel and the breakfast bar where it protruded into the main living room. A good chunk of the carpet was covered with a canvas drop cloth, and newspaper was taped to the glass patio door and all the woodwork to protect it from splatters. In one corner was a stepladder with a clean new paint roller and a couple of brushes balanced across the top step. In the precise center of the room was an old table, draped in plastic, with a selection of paintbrushes and rollers lined up in a row. Near the breakfast bar was a pyramid built of a dozen neatly stacked paint containers, and an open can sat nearby. He'd been contemplating the wall, just about to make the first brush stroke, when he'd heard the noise outside and seized the excuse to get down off the ladder.

He saw Delainey's gaze focus on the paint pyramid and watched as her eyes widened with shock. No doubt she was calculating how much that pile of cans was going to set her back, Sam thought.

"The trouble with a floor plan like this one is that once you start painting there's nowhere to stop," he said. "I bought twelve gallons of paint...and even that may not be enough to finish. That's why I'm so glad to have help to put it on." He looked directly at Curtis and Jason, who were still wedged in the doorway. "That *is* why you've come, isn't it? To paint?"

Jason looked coldly at him. "Surely you're joking. I just

need to give Delainey these figures to work on and we'll get out of your way.''

Sam watched Jason look around for a safe place to lay his notebook. Finally, for lack of another option, he settled on the table in the center of the room where Sam had arranged his extra tools. Jason pushed the brushes aside with his fingertips to clear a space—so careful when he touched them that Sam figured he was afraid one might leap up into his hand and stick.

Too bad I don't have an open paint can sitting right there, he thought idly. It might just—accidentally, of course—spill all over Jason's expensive tasseled loafers.

Sam climbed the ladder, dipped his paintbrush, and looked thoughtfully at the wall. Once he made the first brush stroke, there would be no turning back. Somebody would have to finish the job—and he had no illusions about who the somebody was likely to be. If there had ever been any doubt that he was the one who'd be stuck, Jason had removed it with this drop-by visit. What was he asking Delainey to do, anyway? From the numbers he was throwing around, it sounded as if she was going to be calculating the national trade deficit for the next three hundred years.

Jason said sharply, ''I thought you were supposed to be painting.''

Sam didn't turn his head. ''I find myself ruminating about how Michelangelo must have felt in the moment before his brush first touched the surface of the Sistine Chapel ceiling. Such an awesome responsibility. I wonder which color he started with.''

Jason snorted. ''That answers my question—you *were* listening to the conversation.''

Careless of me to answer at all, Sam thought. On a whim, instead of starting methodically in the corner as he'd intended to do, he leaned toward the space above the mantel and drew an enormous heart shape. The creamy white paint stood out nicely against the faded beige of the wall, but the heart was a little lopsided, with one hump larger than the other. No surprise there—he'd never been able to cut a paper valentine heart right, either. They always came out too skinny.

He surveyed the shape and painted a little swirl at the bottom to smooth out the drips which had run down from the bottom point.

Jason finished explaining to Delainey what he needed and took one more look around the town house. "What a pity you can't afford to hire a professional," he sniffed. "This guy can't even paint a heart straight."

With a flourish, Sam inscribed Delainey's initials under his own inside the heart, and leaned back to admire his work. "It's not supposed to be straight. Notice the artistic little curve at the bottom, which I find somewhat reminiscent of the distorted primary images often used by Miró during his—"

Jason rolled his eyes. "Hey, Delainey, here's a plan. With your guy here whipping the place into shape, you can host the office Christmas party next weekend. You'll have all new paint by then—maybe—and you definitely have plenty of room. We'll just put on the invitation, *Bring Your Own Chair.*" He laughed. "Hear that one, Curtis? Bring your own chair?"

Curtis had wandered away from the table and was standing near the foot of the stairs, looking up.

Delainey's voice caught. "The Christmas party? Jason, I don't think—"

Jason shrugged. "It's always been at RJ's house. With him sick, what do you suggest we do instead?"

"Have it at a hotel."

"They were all booked months ago."

Sam added an arrow to the heart. "Sounds like a great idea to me, honey."

The look she shot at him should have turned him to cinders.

"It'll be your first party in the new house." *And you don't want Jason to guess that you think it'll be the last one.* "You can start the place off right. Begin a tradition."

She obviously got the point. "I'll see how the painting's going and talk to you about the party on Monday, Jason."

"And if I'm not done painting before the party," Sam said as he added feathers to the end of his painted arrow, "we'll tell everybody to dress casual, bring a brush, and pitch in."

Jason sneered. "Funny. Don't forget I'll need those numbers first thing Monday, Delainey."

Sam was surprised that she actually waited till the lights of the Mercedes had faded around the bend in the road before she turned on him. "Thanks a bunch, Wagner."

Sam ignored the sarcasm dripping from her voice. "You're welcome, darling."

She looked stunned. "And precisely what do you think you did that's so great? Thanks to you, now I'm saddled with a party, too."

"Oh, the party's nothing. Turn it over to Gran—she'll have a ball and you won't have to do a thing. She's got it half planned anyway. I thought you were thanking me for convincing Curtis he doesn't want to live at White Oaks after all. Did you see the way his face wrinkled up as he looked around? The man looked like a prune."

"Didn't it occur to you that I didn't want them to come in and get a good view of the place?"

"Why not? Get it out of the way, and Curtis won't have any excuse to come back. What is there to see, anyway? An almost-empty town house, waiting to be painted before the furniture's moved in. Big deal."

"It's what they wouldn't have seen if they'd looked around too closely that would have been the problem."

Sam frowned. "Like what?"

"Hasn't it occurred to you that they might have expected to see something that belonged to you? Clothes, maybe? A fishing rod? Or—here's a news flash—a computer and a whole lot of blank paper? Since you are supposed to be writing a book—''

"But darling, why should they assume, just because we're engaged, that we're living together?" He thought for a minute that he'd silenced her altogether. It gave him quite a jolt of satisfaction. "Of course you seem to have made the same assumption. So if what you're really saying is that *you* want me to move in—''

Delainey took a deep breath and Sam braced himself. But instead of the diatribe he expected, she said, "Just don't let them catch you going home."

Sam shrugged. "I'd tell them I was just visiting my grandmother."

"Who happens to live right next door. Don't you think that sounds a little coincidental?"

"Of course not. She's the one who brought us together, remember? So romantic of dear old Gran to introduce us." He dropped a kiss on Delainey's nose. "Besides, why would I bother keeping my computer here? All they have to do is get one look at that bed of yours, and they won't have any doubt where I like to spend my time when I come to visit."

And then he ducked, knowing if he didn't get out of the way—and fast—she'd probably pick up a paint can and throw it at him.

Much as she would have liked to tell Sam to quit painting so she could work, Delainey knew she didn't dare. He was doing what she'd asked him to do, so even if he chose to do it at odd hours, she was in no position to complain.

She pushed the plastic a little further back from the square foot of the breakfast bar where she'd balanced her notebook computer and stared at the figures Jason had given her. She didn't recognize the specific numbers, but there was something about the whole package which seemed oddly familiar. Was it one of RJ's projects—perhaps one he'd told her about before his illness?

Finally, however, she couldn't concentrate anymore. She put down her pencil and pushed her stool back from the breakfast bar. "Sam, do you have to sound as if you're having the most fun of your life?"

He turned around on the stepladder to look down at her. "Poor darling. If you're jealous, I can find you a brush."

"Yeah, there's no shortage. You have two hands—why do you need twenty-five brushes and rollers?"

"Hey, a craftsman needs his tools—and each one of these has its specialized use. Take this one, for instance. The angled row of bristles helps hold—"

"I'm sorry I asked. I'm trying to work here, all right? Having you whistling—and off key, at that—makes it a little difficult."

He nodded sadly. "I admit, it's a bad habit of mine when I'm trying to cheer myself up. I could try growling if you'd rather."

"How about trying peace and quiet?" She leaned back to survey the work he'd done so far. *If you could call it work,* she thought.

He was still making his way down the longest side of the living room. Patches of the wall, each spot several square feet in area, had disappeared under fresh, gleaming white paint. But in between the patches...

Delainey said, "I was sort of hoping you'd paint the whole room white, you know."

"Really?" He stood back for a better look. "How very dull."

He'd divided the wall into sections with the wide, neat patches he'd painted, and in between he'd used the original beige as a background canvas, creating slap-dash imitations of well-known artists' styles. She had no trouble spotting the Mondrian, though its geometric forms were set off by white dividers rather than the artist's usual black ones.

There was a Seurat-like landscape consisting of white dots in varying sizes, dabbed against the tan background—so many dots that it made her think of a blizzard. And he'd just finished painting a pitchfork next to the white-outlined silhouette of what must be intended to look like a farmer.

I have an albino American Gothic coming to life on my wall.

"It's too bad Picasso didn't have a white period," she said. "Or did he?"

Sam shrugged. "You couldn't prove it by me."

"Hey, it's a little late for you to claim ignorance here. Where'd you learn so much about art, anyway?"

"Gran dragged me to all the museums when I was a kid. And don't go accusing me of being an expert on the art world—because if you didn't know a thing or two about it yourself, you wouldn't recognize the styles. You'd think I was only smearing paint around for the fun of it."

"And you aren't?" Delainey said dryly. "I'm so glad to know that. Are you planning to cover those up eventually?"

"My masterpieces?" He sounded horrified. "You asked me to paint the town house. You didn't specify how I should do it."

"I didn't think I needed to spell out that my reason for choosing white is that it makes a nice background to hang things on."

"But this way, you won't ever need to hang anything."

"My very own art gallery," she mused.

He dipped his brush again and began to paint the outline of a woman's head and shoulders next to the pitchfork. "Just think what it will add to the value of the town house when you sell it. Would you like me to leave a few sections for you to play with?"

"No, thanks—I'm a little busy tonight."

"I noticed that." He painted a pair of glasses on the

farmer. "What was it Jason wanted tonight, anyway? A complete analysis of Whittington's next takeover target?"

"Something like that. Besides, my efforts at creating art would look like finger-painting next to yours."

Sam's face brightened. "Finger-painting—there's a thought."

Delainey bit her tongue, but it was too late. When would she learn?

But Sam seemed to think better of it and stopped short of dipping his hand into the paint can. "Great idea," he mused, "but it would be too much effort to clean it out from under my fingernails. Where did you learn to concentrate like that?"

Did he actually think she'd been so absorbed in her work she hadn't even noticed what he was doing? "Working as a bank teller teaches you to focus on what's in front of you and not even hear what the customer at the next window is asking."

"How long did you have to practice?"

"I started as a trainee when I was still in high school, and I worked all the way through college. Different branches all across the city, but with the same bank."

"And then you just stayed on after graduation."

She smiled a little. "Well, by that time I'd been on the staff so long I had seniority and it didn't make sense to start over somewhere else. Sam—what were you looking for when you upset those files?"

"I wondered how long it would take you to ask. Or for that matter, to give up."

"You're not going to tell me, are you?"

He glanced at her over his shoulder. "I can't." He started to whistle again, more softly this time, and then broke off. "I've got it—I know how you can have all the peace and quiet you want."

Delainey felt panic sweep over her. "You can't leave now," she protested.

"I didn't say I was going home. I'll just take my paint can to another room and start there. It'll make the job seem to go faster."

Delainey gritted her teeth. "No—let's keep this down to one mess at a time. Tell you what—I'm going up to my bedroom to work." She picked up the laptop and the pages of notes Jason had left.

Sam didn't move, but she felt his gaze follow her as she climbed the stairs and she deliberately let her hips sway. He'd told her that sleeping with him wouldn't be adequate payment for the work she wanted him to do—well, if that was how he felt it was just fine with her. She'd made it plain she wasn't interested, no matter what he wanted. But she didn't see any reason to make it easy on him.

Delainey paused in the doorway of her bedroom. The room was dim and cool, and the big bed, with its four carved posts reaching almost to the ceiling, looked solid and reliable. The billowing white lace of the canopy, not only draping the bed but pooling on the carpet, seemed to reach out to her in a cloud of comfort.

Suddenly exhaustion and frustration swept over her and all she wanted to do was nestle deep under the thick comforter and pretend that none of this was happening.

Or, since pretending was going to be a bit difficult, maybe she'd just stop trying to tread water and let herself sink into the puddle of self-pity. Everything she had worked so hard and so long to accomplish was gone. So many years of work, and now her dream was shattered, her career had been run off the rails, her life was in shards. Why shouldn't she feel sorry for herself?

She tossed her papers and the computer onto the comforter and curled up at the head of the bed, leaning against the frilly lace pillow shams. She hadn't bothered to turn on the lamps, so the computer screen was the only light in the room.

Not quite ruined, she reminded herself. *Not yet. Don't jump to conclusions.*

Though the threat was hanging heavy over her head, she hadn't actually lost anything yet. In any case, even if Jason managed to fire her and she had to sell the town house, she wouldn't have lost everything she'd worked for. She still had her education, and she had ten years of valuable experience. There were many other things she could do—maybe even some she'd like better than banking.

What was it she'd told Sam tonight, about how she'd ended up in her present career? *I'd been on the staff so long I had seniority and it didn't make sense to start over somewhere else.*

The fact was, she was a banker today because of inertia—because she'd simply stayed on instead of looking around for a different field all those years ago. Maybe being pushed out of the cozy nest she'd always had at National City would be a good thing in the long run.

Even if she did feel pretty lousy about it at the moment.

She heard footsteps on the stairs and instinctively pulled the computer onto her lap, staring at the spreadsheet on the screen without seeing the numbers. She looked up with a scowl when Sam loomed in the doorway.

"Why no lights?" he asked. "You'll ruin your eyes trying to work that way. I came up to tell you I'm going home, but…oh, my goodness, this looks comfortable. I'm sure you don't mind, since there's plenty of room."

"I mind," Delainey said, as soon as she realized what he intended to do.

But it was too late. Sam had already flung himself across the bed and was sprawled on his back across the width of the mattress near the foot. His arms were flung wide, and he looked totally relaxed. "There's nowhere comfortable to sit downstairs," he said.

"And whose fault is that? You covered up the futon. Sam, if you don't mind—"

"Careful, honey. You don't want me to start wondering whether I'm making you nervous just by sitting on your bed."

"You're not sitting," Delainey pointed out.

But Sam wasn't listening. "Such an unusual bed," he mused. He was staring up at the gold ring mounted to the ceiling at the precise center of the canopy, supporting the lace as it drifted down around the heavily carved posts. "It's especially inviting in the dark. The lace flowing down all around us makes me think of a sheikh's tent somewhere in a lonely desert. The lights are barely glowing, there's a sandstorm howling outside, and I have a willing slave girl awaiting my pleasure…"

His voice wrapped around her as softly as silk thread, and for an instant Delainey was bemused enough to picture the scene exactly as he was describing it. There was something primitively erotic about a tent closing out the storm outside, isolating a man and a woman who basked in warm soft light and in sensual enjoyment of each other…

She must have made a sound, because Sam sat up. "You're not a willing slave girl? That's a pity. Oh, I realize now that I wasn't hearing a howling sandstorm either—that was just you expressing your annoyance at me."

Delainey caught her breath. *The problem with silk thread,* she told herself, *is that if you're surrounded by enough of it, you find yourself caught in a cocoon.* She was lucky she'd come to her senses in time. She frowned at him. "Have you finished with the fantasies, Sam?"

"Oh, no—I'm only getting warmed up. I won't waste them on you, though, since you don't seem to share the enjoyment." He sobered. "The fact that you've never been without a job must make it seem even scarier right now."

Delainey nodded. The motion felt jerky as if something in her neck wasn't working right. "Not since I was seventeen. All through college, through a dozen roommates, through losing my parents…it's always been the one thing that stayed the same. Different jobs, of course, and different branches—but always National City.''

Sam slid off the bed.

She told herself she was glad he was going, but something deep inside her wanted to ask him not to leave her alone right now. A perfectly silly notion, of course. She'd always been alone. She liked being alone. And in the present circumstances, she'd positively prefer being alone... wouldn't she?

Instead of leaving, however, he moved to perch on the side of the bed near the pillows, right next to her. Delainey tensed, and Sam shook his head. ''I'm not trying to seduce you.''

''Smart of you not to attempt the impossible.''

''Careful. That sounded almost like a challenge.'' He pulled a pillow from behind her. ''Slide around with your back to me.''

Suddenly—she wasn't quite sure how—she was cradled against him, her spine against his chest. Gently, his hands brushed over her hair and then settled at the base of her neck with each fingertip pressing gently into her scalp at the hairline. Slowly and gently, his fingers moved upward, each tracing a path through her hair, massaging the scalp, until his hands met and his fingers laced on the top of her head. Then he pulled back and started once more at the nape of her neck.

Delainey's head drooped forward. She tried to hold it up straight, but she couldn't seem to. ''You know you're ruining my hair.''

Sam obviously recognized it for the token protest it was, because he didn't even pause. ''So sue me.''

''Remind me whenever you're done, and I will.'' Her voice felt heavy.

With each stroke of his hands, every finger took a slightly different path, wandering over her head until each square inch had been gently rubbed and soothed.

She felt limp, enervated. Though he was massaging only her scalp, her entire body felt totally relaxed, as if the sensations roused by his fingers had trickled out through every nerve and found their way to each individual cell.

She was completely relaxed—and yet stimulated in a way that was unlike anything she'd ever felt before. She'd had no idea until now that her scalp was an erogenous zone—particularly the square inch just above her right ear, which he seemed to be particularly fond of.

Because every nerve was vibrating, it took her a moment to realize that he'd stopped—and even then she couldn't immediately force herself to move. She sat, her head drooped, as he pushed the heavy weight of her hair up and away and kissed the nape of her neck, a long, slow, tender caress.

"You were complaining about your hairdo?" Sam whispered.

"Yeah." Delainey's voice felt rough. "This is your last warning—do that again and I'll make you pay for sure."

He laughed. "If I do it again, sweetheart, you'll be asleep."

Not likely. The odds were far greater that she'd lean back against him, turn her head, let her lips brush his cheek… *Talk about asking for trouble… No, screaming for trouble would be a better description.*

"Thanks," she said, trying to keep her tone crisp. "That was…quite pleasant. A very nice way to unwind." She pulled the computer closer, as if it was body armor. "Now I really do need to—"

"Delainey," he interrupted. "Have you eaten anything today?"

"I don't remember." As if prompted by the question, her stomach growled. "Apparently not."

"Sit tight. I'll see what I can find."

What happened to the idea of you going home? she wanted to ask. But he was gone.

She did her best to focus on the spreadsheet displayed on her computer, but her ability to concentrate was shattered. All she could think of was the way his fingers had felt as they arched through her hair, at first very gently but with increasing boldness and pressure as she grew accustomed to his touch, and then gentling once more...

A voice in the back of her brain murmured, *That's probably how he makes love, too. Very, very gently, until you want more and more and—*

"Oh, shut up!" she told herself irritably. She took a deep breath and stared at the computer screen. Why did these numbers sound so familiar?

Maybe, she thought, it wasn't because this was something from RJ's files. Maybe it was because she'd put them together herself.

With a couple of clicks, she pulled up another spreadsheet. It was one she hadn't looked at for nearly a week, one that was still on her computer only because she'd neglected to clear it off.

She put the two sets of numbers side by side, and bit her lip while she looked at them for a while. Then she pushed the computer aside and leaned back into the pillows, closing her eyes to think.

She didn't know how long it had been when she heard a rustle from the doorway. She sat up. "Sam?"

"I thought you were asleep." He set down a tray that held two big mismatched mugs and a stack of crackers still in the waxed paper wrapper.

"No, just thinking."

"About sheep, right?"

"No, about takeover targets."

"What's Curtis going to be acquiring this time?" He handed her a spoon and sat down opposite the tray. "It's only vegetable soup from a can. But since the can was in your pantry, I'm sure it's the kind you like best."

"Why do you want to know what Curtis is after?"

His eyebrows raised. "Suspicious, aren't we? I was just making conversation. If you don't want to talk about that, then how about giving me some ideas for making up with your secretary?"

"Oh, I'm sure you'll think of something."

He shrugged. "Maybe I'll just give her a scalp massage."

Delainey, still preoccupied with her discovery, said absently, "If you did, her husband would come after you with a shotgun."

Sam paused with his spoon halfway to his mouth, while the seconds stretched to half a minute.

"What?" Delainey said finally. "What's wrong with you?"

"All I did was rub your head, Delainey. I find it interesting that you seem to think it was an intimate experience."

Delainey opened her mouth, and shut it again. Because what could she say that wouldn't give him an even bigger boost to the ego?

"Thanks for telling me," Sam murmured. "That's very, *very* nice to know."

Sam was already at work when she came downstairs in the morning, dressed in her oldest clothes and with her hair tied back in a hasty ponytail. "You're the picture of an artist at work," he said cheerfully as she rounded the bottom of the stairs. "The coffee's already made." His roller made a soft, squishy hiss against the wall.

Delainey stopped dead, staring at the long wall where he'd been creating his cartoon masterpieces last night. The drawings were gone, forever buried under solid, gleaming white. When had he had time to do all that, she wondered. Last night while she'd been upstairs trying to work through the trickle of self-pity? Or had he been up before dawn this morning?

"I guess I don't need to ask what happened to the key I left with Emma that day the bed was delivered," she said finally. "I don't know why I didn't think of it last night, when you were already inside when I got home."

"You were preoccupied." He dipped his roller again.

"And you've been busy." She pointed at the heart above the mantelpiece, the only segment of his playful brushwork to survive. "Did you overlook that one, or are you planning to leave it?"

"I didn't have the heart to paint it out."

Delainey groaned. "It's much too early in the morning for puns, Wagner."

"Have some coffee and you'll feel better." The doorbell rang. "That's probably Gran bringing muffins—she was stirring them up when I left."

It was indeed Emma at the door, but she wasn't carrying muffins. She looked past Delainey to Sam and said, "Liz is on the phone. She sounded quite upset, but she wouldn't tell me what was wrong. She wants to talk to you."

Sam stepped back from the wall to admire his handiwork.

"She said she's in Cancún," Emma said.

Sam looked vaguely interested. "She's supposed to be on a cruise ship in the middle of the Gulf of Mexico."

"Well, she's not. Since I didn't know Delainey's number, I told her I'd come and get you. That's a hint, in case you missed it, Sam. She's waiting."

"Knowing Liz, the crisis will be over before I get there anyway."

Delainey couldn't stop herself. "To Cancún?"

"No. To the phone." Sam put down the roller and went out. He didn't appear to be in any hurry.

"Who's Liz?" Delainey tried to sound casual. "A girl-friend?"

"Oh no," Emma said cheerfully.

Delainey told herself it was crazy to be relieved. Or, for

that matter, to have been curious in the first place. It was none of her business.

"Not for quite a while now," Emma went on. "She's a nice girl, though."

So Liz was not just an ex-girlfriend, Delainey thought, but a nice ex-girlfriend who called him up from Cancún with a problem....

And why should it matter to you? the inconvenient little voice in the back of her brain murmured. *Why should you expect to be the first damsel in distress that Sam's rescued? Or the last?*

She dipped a brush and began to touch up a couple of spots where the white paint didn't seem to have entirely covered the beige.

"That's an endless job," Emma said. "Patching up the streaks, I mean. I'm afraid you'll find that it's just too big a space for paint to look good. You might think about breaking it up with some wallpaper."

Or some original art, Delainey thought. Now that the albino American Gothic was forever gone, she found herself remembering it—particularly the pitchfork—with fondness.

"Something like Liz did next door."

Delainey's hand jerked, the brush flew out of her fingers, and white paint splattered across the carpet in a neat arc.

"I'm not wild about purple and hunter green, it's true," Emma mused. "They're a little bright for my taste. But the idea of visually dividing the spaces with different papers and borders—"

Delainey's mind flashed back to the day she'd visited Emma. She remembered noticing the vibrant colors on the walls and in the furniture. And she remembered being surprised that Emma had chosen those things, because they hadn't seemed quite like the older woman's style.

But Emma *hadn't* chosen the color palette, or even approved it. Liz had. Liz—the ex-girlfriend.

Delainey said faintly, "But I thought it was your town house, Emma."

"Mine? And you thought Sam was living with me? Oh, no, dear. I'm just a guest."

"Then…it's Sam's?" Delainey couldn't quite understand why her voice seemed to have a crack in it. So what if his ex-girlfriend had decorated his town house? He'd probably left it alone because it was too much bother to change it.

"Actually, no," Emma said. "To be precise, it belongs to Liz."

CHAPTER SEVEN

DELAINEY'S head was swimming. If the town house belonged to Liz, and Emma was staying there as a guest... Then was she Liz's guest, or Sam's? Or—more likely—both?

Sam's living with Liz.

She didn't want to believe it, but the conclusion was inescapable.

Or was it? The town house next door was larger than her own. Delainey had noticed the day she visited Emma to take her the roses that it was one of the three-bedroom units in the complex. So perhaps Sam was just Liz's guest too, she told herself. There would be enough room...

But she had to admit that idea was improbable in the extreme. A very good pal might possibly invite her jobless male friend to move into her guest room for a while. But to ask his grandmother to come and stay with them... No. That went way beyond the bounds of friendship.

Stop grasping at straws and admit the truth, Delainey. He's sleeping with her.

But if they were together, why was Liz in Cancún? She was supposed to be on a cruise, Sam had said. So why wasn't he there with her?

Delainey could think of a dozen reasons, and not a one of them threw any doubt on her original conclusion.

Emma snapped her fingers suddenly. The sound startled Delainey, who'd been so caught up in her own thoughts she'd forgotten the woman was still there.

"I knew I was missing something," Emma said. "I left the muffins in the oven, and Sam will never hear the buzzer."

Because he'll be too involved with Liz's problem, whatever it is, even to hear an oven timer go off.

Emma scurried away. The front door didn't quite close behind her.

Delainey belatedly noticed the splotches of paint on the carpet where her brush had landed, so she got a roll of paper towels and a bucket of water and began trying to mop them up. Her head was still buzzing with shock. If Emma's oven timer had gone off in her ear instead of next door, Delainey probably wouldn't have been able to hear it.

And the more she replayed the conversation—and the argument with herself—in her head, the more confused she got. Emma had distinctly said that Liz wasn't Sam's girlfriend, and that she hadn't been for quite a while. Delainey had assumed, of course, that she'd meant they'd broken up—but Emma must simply have been saying that because they'd taken the next step deeper into the relationship by moving in together, *girlfriend* wasn't quite the right title anymore.

But Emma knew about the engagement. Didn't it bother her that her grandson was living with one woman—even if she happened to be out of the country at the moment—but at the same time was engaged to another?

Of course not, Delainey thought. She'd asked Sam herself whether he'd explained to Emma that the engagement was a farce, and he'd reassured her. *Gran knows it's not serious,* Sam had told her. *She's a romantic, not an idiot.*

Delainey's head hurt.

The front door swung wide and Sam came in. "Well, that creates a bit of inconvenience." He seemed quite cheerful.

"Really." Delainey didn't intend it to sound like a question.

"Liz is flying home from Cancún tomorrow."

Tomorrow? "I can see where that might cause you a

little concern.'' She didn't even try to keep the sarcastic edge out of her voice.

Sam shot a look at her, eyebrows raised. ''Since she wasn't supposed to be home for two more weeks, yes, it's a bit of a pain.''

Delainey remembered Sam asking her how long she thought it would be before she knew whether her job was safe, and when she'd mentioned a month, he'd said that would be difficult. No wonder he'd jumped at the chance when she'd suggested they make things look good for a couple of weeks and then stage a huge fight....

But now, even another week would be too long to keep up the pretense. Six whole days too long—because Liz was coming home tomorrow.

Now Delainey's stomach was hurting too.

''Nice of her to at least warn you,'' she said finally. *Or maybe she's realized from previous experience that she needs to give notice so you can tidy up all the unfinished business before she gets home.*

''That's true. I'll have to thank her for being thoughtful—though that's not why she called.''

The drops of paint Delainey was trying to wipe up were smearing further instead of lifting out of the carpet fibers. Where there had been a dozen large splotches, there was now a foot-wide white smudge. Her hands felt weak and shaky, and finally in frustration she threw the paper towel down and stomped on it. ''The hell with it,'' she said. ''The carpet has to be replaced anyway. Why bother?''

Sam looked startled. ''What's your problem?''

If he didn't get it all by himself, Delainey thought, there was absolutely no point in trying to explain. ''Nothing,'' she snapped.

''Here, you're just making it worse. Let me do that.'' He dropped to one knee next to the spot, dampened a fresh paper towel from her bucket, and started to methodically work the paint from the edges of the smear back toward the middle.

As if, Delainey thought, he didn't have a single other important thing on his mind. Finally she couldn't stand the silence anymore. "I don't suppose it ever occurred to you to mention Liz to me."

He didn't look up. "Didn't see any reason to."

That certainly puts you in your place, Hodges. "Well, her coming home early might be what you call an inconvenience, but I'd consider it a calamity myself."

He stopped wiping for a moment. "Why is it a calamity for you?"

"I didn't mean for me. I meant if I was you, I'd... Oh, never mind. I just think you'd be plenty worried about having to explain to her than you've gotten yourself technically engaged to me."

"Wait a minute. What do you mean, I got myself engaged to you? You were the one doing all the engaging, as I recall."

He was right—though admitting the mess was all her own fault didn't make Delainey feel any better. "How it happened isn't the point now. But it's not exactly a secret, so you're going to have to tell Liz."

"I already have. You have the distinction of having taken her mind off her own troubles for slightly over a minute—something of a world's record. And as for the rest of it—well, I've been homeless before."

The paint smear was growing smaller by the second.

Delainey wasn't sure she'd heard him right. He hadn't sounded like a man talking about the most important woman in his life. On the other hand, it couldn't be more obvious that Liz hadn't reacted very well, so no wonder he sounded irritated. "Homeless?" Her voice felt very small. "You mean you really think she'll throw you out?"

"Oh, no—she won't ask me to leave. In fact, she'll probably beg me to stay in the hope it'll make Jack jealous."

Delainey's head was pounding. "Who's Jack?"

"The husband she had a fight with on the cruise. The reason she got off the ship in Cancún. The cause of her coming home two weeks early. Anything else you want to know?"

He *wasn't* living with Liz? Liz was married—to someone else? Delainey took a step backward and kicked a paint can.

"Watch out there," Sam said mildly. "I'm just getting this spot cleaned up, and I really don't want another one to deal with."

"Sorry." She set the can at a safer distance.

"At any rate, since I'd just as soon not deal with a jealous Jack," Sam went on, "I'll be officially homeless as of tomorrow when I pick Liz up at the airport."

Things were finally falling into place. Delainey couldn't believe it had taken her so long to catch on. "You've been house-sitting."

"If you want to be technical, I've been cat-sitting. The Empress has convinced Liz that she's far too aristocratic to be boarded, so whenever Liz leaves town someone has to move in to take care of the cat. Now that I've gotten to know her better, I believe the truth is that the Empress has exhausted the patience of every cat-boarding facility in the city and has been asked never to return, but—"

"You kept saying she wasn't your cat." Relief surged through Delainey, followed by a wave of confusion over why she should be feeling so relieved. Yes, it had been shaping up to be a heck of a muddle, but it wasn't like the whole engagement thing was real. And even if it had been, she wasn't the one who'd been two-timing Liz—it was Sam's problem. So why was she feeling so much better all of a sudden?

"It's a habit," Sam said. "Almost a reflex, because I want to make sure no one thinks that ill-mannered animal actually belongs to me."

"I thought you meant she was Emma's."

"You thought…" He wadded up the last paper towel and arched it toward the wastebasket. "You thought I was messing around behind Liz's back."

"Well…yes. *No*—I mean, you haven't been messing around. Nothing's happened between us."

"Not yet," Sam said.

Delainey decided to ignore him. "It's just that—well, you are sort of engaged to me, and I naturally thought it would be a little awkward if…" She saw him start to smile and concluded that she was only digging herself in deeper. "Where do you live? I mean, when you're not cat-sitting."

"I told you, I'm officially homeless at the moment. My lease was up about the time Liz and Jack were leaving, so when I agreed to look after the Empress I didn't renew it. I thought putting up with a cat for three months would be no trick at all."

"Three months? Where have they been?"

"Jack's an attorney. His doctor told him to either take a break from the hectic schedule or figure out how to fit a heart attack into his calendar, so—Jack being Jack—he signed on with a cruise company to be their resident lawyer. He's been sailing the Caribbean ever since, moving from one ship to another every couple of weeks, keeping office hours on the sundeck to advise all the wealthy patrons about tax shelters and trust funds."

"And Liz went with him?"

"She writes software—which she can do from anywhere."

An attorney and a computer engineer, Patty had told her on the day she'd first looked at the town house, when they'd been talking about her prospective neighbors. After meeting Sam and Emma, Delainey had assumed that either Patty had been mistaken or she'd been referring to the people who lived in the unit around the corner.

Reminded of Emma, she asked, "But what about your grandmother? How does she fit into all this?"

"Gran put her house up for sale in the autumn so she could move into an apartment in the new retirement center they're building downtown. But the house sold faster than she expected it to, and she's still waiting for her apartment to be finished. It's supposed to be done before Christmas, though, so she won't be sleeping in a cardboard box for long."

Delainey took that one with a grain of salt. "She can come and stay with me."

"Gran will never run short of options. In fact, she says she only moved in here in the first place to protect Liz's house from me." He sounded almost hurt.

"But what will you do until you find another place to live?"

"Oh, I've found one."

"Well, that's good. Unless you mean you're moving away—because I really do need you for a few more days, Sam."

"No problem. I'll be here." Sam stood up and looked around as if he was seeing the town house for the first time.

Suddenly Delainey was getting a queasy feeling in the pit of her stomach. "When you say *here,*" she said uneasily, "you mean you're staying in the city—right?"

"I mean I'm staying right here," Sam went on. "Last night you said you were afraid of what would happen if Jason and Curtis came in and didn't see any of my stuff scattered around. Now you won't have to worry any more, sweetheart, because I'll just move in with you."

On Sunday morning, Sam packed up everything he'd brought with him and carried his two big suitcases around the corner to Delainey's town house. "I figured it would be easier to have the move out of the way before Liz gets home," he said when she opened the door.

To his disappointment, she didn't even swallow hard. "Oh, I quite agree. This is much better than playing out a scene with you packing while Liz is down on her knees begging you to stay. Though perhaps that would be more soothing to your ego."

He patted her briskly on the top of the head. "I'm proud of you, Delainey. You barely even sounded sarcastic."

"I'll try harder next time. You can put your stuff in the back bedroom."

He carried the suitcases upstairs and stood in the doorway of the back bedroom for a long moment, looking thoughtfully at the pile of boxes which lined one wall. For a woman who had basically no furniture, he thought, she sure owned a lot of stuff.

When he came downstairs again, Delainey was in the kitchen, scrubbing yesterday's coffee mugs. The coffeemaker was sighing as if in relief as it finished the cycle.

"What's in all those boxes up there?" he asked.

She sighed as if she didn't like being reminded. "Things I need to sort out. Some of it's from my parents' house— I just packed things up because I didn't have time to go through everything right then. It's all been in storage since they died, because I've never found time to do it."

"Household stuff?"

"Some, but mostly it's papers and documents. They kept everything. The trouble is most of it's worthless, but I can't just throw it all away—I'll have to look at every scrap of paper first."

"And you get enough of that kind of detail work on the job to make you feel ill at the idea of doing it on your free time."

She nodded. "Then there's a bunch of stuff that I really need to just throw out. Textbooks and notes and test papers. I kept everything till I was finished with college, in case I needed to go back to look something up. But it took me so long to finish my education that I'd gotten sort of attached to it all by then. Silly, of course."

"It took longer because you had to work your way through school, right? Your parents were dead by then?"

"No, but they thought a degree was a waste of time, when I could keep right on being a bank teller without one."

"The pinnacle of success," he murmured.

She smiled a little. "So I was a nontraditional student. I commuted for a while from the little town where I grew up, then I found a roommate and moved to the city and transferred to a bigger branch of the bank, and drove back and forth across town between job and classes. It took six years. Coffee?"

Obviously she didn't intend to talk about it anymore. He could understand that, because he could hear the pain of those years, faint but still real, in the undertones of her voice. She was right—it was time for a change of subject. He reached for the coffeepot. "We'll have to move some of the boxes in order to fit in a bed of some sort. Unless you're inviting me to move into your room."

She didn't miss a beat. "You can sleep on the futon."

"And take the chance of Jason or Curtis dropping by at an odd hour and catching me? You're the one who was worried about what they might see—or not see."

"I guess that means you'll have to be up every morning at the crack of dawn. It'll be good for you."

"But that bed of yours is large enough to sleep three. Not that I'm trying to sound kinky. I'm just stating the facts."

"But you said sleeping with you wouldn't be adequate pay for all this work." She made a sweeping gesture that took in both the newly painted walls and the ones that still stood out stark beige.

"Oh, what I'm suggesting doesn't have anything to do with pay," Sam assured her. "It would be just pure fun. Trust me."

*   *   *

By Sunday afternoon, the entire lower level of the town house, except for the heart Sam had painted above the mantel, gleamed white. So painfully white, in fact, with nothing breaking up the expanse of walls, that it almost hurt Delainey's eyes. "It doesn't exactly look like a good place to hold a party," she muttered. "But what kind of excuse am I going to make to Jason for why I don't want to have it here?" Then she tapped her knuckles on her forehead. "Dummy—you don't need an excuse. You just say no, that's all."

Sam folded up the stepladder and set it at the bottom of the stairs, ready to carry up. "Why say no? Have the party."

"Give me one good reason."

"Just make it *your* party, not Jason's."

"You mean, if it's the only party I'm going to have here, make it a memorable one?"

"That's the general idea." He picked up the ladder and carried it upstairs.

Delainey thought it over while she cleared away the plastic and newspaper downstairs. By the time she was finished moving the furniture back in place and relocating the clock on the mantel and her other few decorations, the town house looked slightly less like an overlighted warehouse.

"You may have been right about my choice of paint colors," she told Sam when he came back downstairs to get rollers and paint cans. "It's pretty bright."

"If you're suggesting I start over with another shade of white, you can forget it."

"No—I'll just have to get some posters or something to break it up."

"Or train yourself to appreciate the nice, clean look. I like it, myself."

"I'll work on it. Sam, didn't you say Liz's plane was due to land at three?"

"No sense in getting in a hurry just so I can kill time at the airport. Do you want to come along when I pick her up?"

She was startled. "You want me to come to the airport with you? Why?"

"Hey, I act as body armor for you—protection against the Curtises of the world. Now's your chance to return the favor."

So much for the warm fuzzy feeling that he actually wanted her company. Still... "Sam, if you expect me to believe that you need protection against someone like the little sweetheart you described to me—"

"Sure I do. If you're along, the little sweetheart won't tell me all her troubles."

"Are you certain of that?"

"Absolutely. She can tell *you* all her troubles, and I won't have to bother to nod and make agreeing noises like I'm actually listening. Everybody will be happy."

"You're a cynic, Sam."

"All right, you force me to confess. What I really need isn't you, it's your car."

"I'm amazed. You're not going to pick Liz up on the motorcycle?"

"I'm afraid it won't tow a trailer big enough to carry all her luggage."

"What about Emma's car?"

"Gran's off socializing. I think she's trying to find a friend who'll feel sorry for her and take her in for a couple of weeks because she's too cheap to stay at a hotel."

"And what will you do if I say I have plans and need my car?"

Sam shrugged. "Hire a limo and give Liz the bill. You don't have to go, you know. You can stay here and move all the boxes out of the back bedroom so I can paint it when I get home."

Home. How easily he used the word. *I'd better watch out or I'll have a permanent houseguest,* she thought.

''As long as you put it that way,'' she said dryly, ''I'll be delighted to come along for the ride.''

Delainey didn't realize that she'd formed a mental picture of Liz Adams until she came face-to-face with the young woman and had to admit that the image and the reality were far from a match.

The young woman who bounded down the escalator to meet them in the airport lobby was small and slender, wearing jeans and headphones, with her blond hair pulled back in a careless ponytail, and when Sam asked about her luggage she pulled a backpack off her shoulder and handed it to him. ''That's it,'' she said. ''Everything else is still on the cruise ship. Let Jack deal with getting it home.''

''He may just throw it overboard,'' Sam observed.

Liz pushed back a lock of hair that had come loose from the ponytail, and the marquise diamond on her left hand flashed fire. ''No. First, as an attorney, he's very sensitive about property destruction and littering laws. Second, since he paid for most of it, he's not going to throw it away. Third, he's totally anal, which is the main reason I'm here instead of there. There's a basic incompatibility in our personalities which makes it fundamentally impossible—''

''—For you to say hello to Delainey,'' Sam interrupted.

Liz blinked. ''Oh. Hi. Sorry to have such a one-track mind.''

''It's understandable,'' Delainey said.

''It's nice to meet you. Sam told me you're partially engaged to him—whatever that means—and if I comment on your ring, I'm dead. So please explain to me how you can be partially engaged—because frankly it sounds like being a little bit pregnant—and what's the deal with the ring?''

"When they handed out tact," Sam said, "Liz was last in line, so she got short-changed."

"It's a perfectly reasonable question," Delainey said. "And I'm not the one who bought the dimestore diamond, so don't expect me to get defensive about it." She held out her left hand.

She would have expected that the harsh fluorescent lights would make the stone look shinier and brighter—but instead it looked worse. Or perhaps it was just being held up next to Liz's flawless marquise that made it seem yellower.

Liz's eyes widened as she took in the sight, and then she looked up at Sam. "Buddy," she said firmly, "you are incredibly cheap." She linked her arm into Delainey's. "I can tell we're going to be great friends. So tell me—what made you settle for such an improbable fiancé as Sam?"

Jason was waiting for her, sitting on the corner of her desk, when Delainey got to work the next morning. "Where have you been?" he demanded. "You're two hours late."

"I told you I was going out to George Laurent's office to look at his books in order to evaluate his loan application."

"I thought I made it clear that was too small a deal to bother with."

"You indicated something of the sort," Delainey agreed. "Though it leaves me wondering how you could make that judgment about a firm you know nothing about."

"What are you implying, Delainey?"

"Nothing. Just curious. I thought your great pal Curtis might have mentioned it, that's all."

"Curtis is too busy to gossip about things like that. He was in this morning, by the way—to set up new accounts."

"How nice for him."

"And for the bank. The initial deposit was five million."

"Well, at that rate he shouldn't have any trouble maintaining the minimum balance to get free checking,'' Delainey murmured. "Here are those figures you wanted me to work through over the weekend.''

He seized the paper from her hand and ran an eye over the numbers.

Delainey watched with interest. "It looks like it would be a good acquisition target for Curtis. Nice core business, solid fundamentals, but not much cash on hand. In fact, it reminded me remarkably of Elmer Bannister's firm, and that made me wonder…''

Jason darted a sideways look at her. "That's not your case anymore.''

"It doesn't mean I'm not still interested. Let's see, the last I knew, you were going to talk to the potential investors I'd suggested and set up a time for us to make a full presentation. How's that going, Jason?''

"They weren't interested.''

She let her eyebrows creep up. "You've talked to all of them already? And none of them even wanted to take a look?''

Jason slid off the corner of her desk. "You'd better decide which side you're on, Delainey. You're already skating on thin ice—watch your step, or you just might fall through.''

When she opened the town house door that evening, Delainey was greeted by the twin smells of roasting beef and freshly cut pine. In the exact center of the living room stood a Christmas tree, half draped in fairy lights, directly atop the spot where the carpet was stained. Nearby was an open box brimming with decorations.

Sam stepped from behind the tree, untangling yet another strand of lights. "Hope you don't mind,'' he said. "If we're going to have this party next weekend we'd better start getting prepared. I found the boxes of decorations when I was moving stuff around in the back bedroom.''

"Didn't you find the box marked *tree?* It should have been right with the others."

"Artificial Christmas trees are like virtual sex."

Delainey had started to take off her coat, but that stopped her. *"What?"*

"Not even in the same league when it comes to sensory experience."

"I see. Well, don't get your hopes up too high."

Sam looked intrigued. "About which one?"

When will you learn to watch what you say? "I meant, don't kill yourself getting ready for the party. We may not be having it after all, because I may not be employed by Saturday night."

Sam shrugged. "In that case we'll really enjoy the party. Want to tell me what happened?"

"Oh, there's this deal I'd put together, only Jason grabbed it—and now instead of following through as I'd intended, I think he's setting the company up to be Curtis's next takeover target. And I think I know what the one after that's going to be too. There's this packaging firm that Foursquare Electronics used—I'm not supposed to be talking about it, though."

"Hey, confidentiality only lasts while they're paying you."

"Well, they're still paying me, so forget I said that, all right? I stopped at the hospital to see RJ. He seems to be doing remarkably well."

"Did you tell him about Jason?"

"I want him to get better, not have another heart attack. He should be out of the hospital in a few days, but of course he won't be back to work for a while. Is that pot roast I smell? You've been busy."

"Very busy. I've been making a list of all the jobs I'm not going to do around the house."

"Really? Is that supposed to explain why there's a big cutting board lying on the countertop?"

"It's not actually a cutting board, it's a heat-proof surface. That was Gran's idea, to cut out the burned spot and put in something that won't scorch. It's obviously the perfect location to set a hot pan, or it wouldn't have gotten damaged in the first place."

"And you're doing this so you can avoid work?"

"Certainly. It's a great deal easier than taking out the whole countertop and starting over."

Delainey could hardly argue that one. "Don't forget to give me the bills."

"I'm keeping them very carefully, close to my heart."

"Speaking of hearts—" She waved a hand toward the mantelpiece. "Are you ever going to paint over that one?"

"I can't bring myself to do it—you'll have to. Go have a bath or something. Dinner will be ready in half an hour."

Meekly, Delainey went off to follow orders. What a change from one of her normal homecomings, she thought. It wouldn't be hard to get used to this sort of treatment.

On the other hand, how long would Sam find it amusing to play househusband? The game was bound to pall. Of course, in the time she'd known him he hadn't shown the least inclination to go hunting for a job, either. He seemed to be quite happy to fiddle around the house, taking care of her...and his own best interests, of course.

But how long would that last—for either of them?

She brought it up over dinner. "How are the job prospects looking these days?"

"I'm pretty fully occupied right now."

"At the moment, yes, with the town house and all. But have you thought long term? Maybe you should consider going back to school."

"Emma must have told you I never finished." He didn't sound concerned. "That's always bothered her."

"I should think it might."

"But if you're suggesting I take up something different,

let me remind you that I already have. I like this writing business. It has a certain aura about it, a kind of mystique.''

''Really?'' Delainey's voice was dry.

Sam grinned. ''Yeah. And just as soon as I think of a topic for this book I'm going to be writing, I'll—''

The doorbell chimed. He raised an eyebrow at Delainey, who shook her head. ''I'm not expecting anyone.''

Sam tossed down his napkin and went to answer it. Delainey got up to clear the plates.

A moment later he came across the living room, but he wasn't alone. Curtis Whittington was following him.

''I see I'm interrupting dinner,'' Curtis said, ''so I won't stay.''

''Downright insightful of you,'' Sam said under his breath.

Curtis looked straight at Delainey. ''I've had inquiries made, and there are no units at White Oaks for sale just now. So I'd like to buy this one. I'll make it worth your while.'' He reached into his pocket and pulled out a checkbook. ''Name your price, Delainey.''

CHAPTER EIGHT

DELAINEY could hardly believe her ears. Had Curtis really said *Name your price?*

He hadn't meant it, of course. Nobody bought property that way, not even the mega-zillionaire merger king—because if he went around tossing out blank checks like that, he wouldn't remain a mega-zillionaire for long.

But it was an almost overwhelming temptation to call his bluff—to pretend to believe him and sing out some outrageous figure about ten times what she'd paid, just for the pleasure of watching while Curtis tried to squirm himself out of his grandiose offer.

But what if instead of squirming, he took her up on it?

Then grab the check, split the profits with Sam, and run, the little voice in the back of her head suggested. With that kind of money—even with her half—she could take her time in looking for another job. She could buy another town house. She could...

But of course, that wasn't what would really happen if she pulled a figure out of the air. If she gave him a price, she'd only be confirming that the town house was for sale, and then Curtis would say something about needing to be realistic, and he'd settle down to hard bargaining. He was, after all, the master of the merger deal. He knew how to negotiate to advantage—his own advantage—and he certainly knew that the first and most necessary step in making a deal was to get the other party to sit down at the table in the beginning. To agree that a deal was even possible.

That was all he was doing right now, getting her to admit that she was willing to haggle over the price of her town house.

Still, the idea of saying goodbye to Curtis at the front door while holding a seven-figure check was a heartwarming picture. Under those circumstances, she could feel positively fond of the guy.

She gave up the image somewhat reluctantly. "That's certainly an interesting proposition," she said. "But I've just moved in. I really don't want to move again."

From the corner of her eye, she caught Sam's sideways look at her. He looked half startled, half irritated.

It's not exactly a lie, she thought in vexation. She didn't *want* to move; she just might not have a choice in the matter. And as for Sam being annoyed with her—what was he upset about, anyway? The fact that she hadn't jumped at the possibility of a sale? Hadn't rattled off some enormous number? As if that would have been the end of the negotiations.

Sam, my sweet, you'd be a lot smarter not to start spending the profits from the town house until you have the cash held tight in your fist, she thought.

"At any rate," she went on, "I wouldn't begin to know how to put a value on my home."

"Don't try that old trick on me," Curtis said flatly. "It hasn't been your home long enough for you to get attached to it, so quit acting coy about your fondness for the place. I'm not paying good money for nostalgia, especially when it's the imaginary kind."

From the perspective of the merger king, she thought, the approach certainly made sense. A good businessman never got so attached to anything that he was unwilling to sell it. Corporations, divisions, employee contracts, stocks, options, town houses, polo ponies...they must all be pretty much the same to Curtis. Just pieces of property with no sentimental value.

"And you can stop playing dumb," Curtis went on, "because of course you know how to set a price. You're a banker. Let's start with what you paid and figure from there.''

Such a charming fellow. So pleasant to be around. Such a way with words.

But he'd confirmed one thing for her—regardless of what he'd said when he first came in, he hadn't actually intended to let her set the price. She hoped Sam was listening closely.

Delainey wouldn't be surprised if Curtis knew to the penny how much she'd paid for the town house. There were public records of things like that, and Curtis had plenty of underlings with nothing better to do than search out whatever mundane information the boss requested.

Curtis said, ''I'll give you twice what you have invested in it.''

Sam said something under his breath that Delainey didn't quite catch. She was pretty sure, however, that the word *cheap* had been in there somewhere, mixed with an uncomplimentary reference to the marital status of Curtis's parents.

She felt like jabbing an elbow into Sam's ribs.

Instead, she smiled as sweetly as she could at Curtis. ''I'll give it some thought and get back to you.''

''All right. Triple what you have invested.''

This was starting to be interesting. ''I'd need to talk to my partner, of course,'' Delainey said, ''before I made any decision that important.''

Curtis seemed to discount that necessity. ''I'll write the check now.'' He flipped open his checkbook, patted his shirt pocket, and looked around vaguely. ''I seem to have lost my pen.''

Delainey had no trouble reading the message. *No pen? So sorry—I can't write the check after all, and that means you've missed your chance.*

Not that she believed for an instant that it was true. This was nothing more than a gimmick intended to make her think hard about the opportunity she'd supposedly passed up. The idea was to soften her up, to make her more amenable to negotiation the next time Curtis approached—and more likely to take a lower offer, rather than lose out entirely.

With a flourish, Sam pulled a ballpoint from his shirt pocket and held it out.

Delainey wanted to kick him. Could he possibly make it any plainer that he was in favor of the deal?

Curtis scribbled a figure on the check and signed his name. Then he laid the checkbook, with the check still attached, in the middle of the breakfast bar where they could all see it clearly.

Delainey didn't need to calculate whether he'd multiplied right; she could tell at a glance that he'd been well-informed about the purchase price.

Curtis didn't take his hand off the checkbook. "For this kind of money, though, I want immediate possession."

For that? Make it plus a million, and I'll think about it. Delainey bit her tongue to keep from saying it and congratulated herself for her restraint. "Sorry, Curtis. Even if we agreed to a deal, I couldn't move out right this minute."

Curtis said, "Why not? I can give you the names of some excellent hotels."

She'd have suspected him of being ironic, if she had ever seen any evidence that the man possessed a sense of humor. "Because we'd be leaving you with the dirty dishes," she said gently, "and that would be unbearably rude. Thanks for dropping by, Curtis. As I said in the first place, I'll give it some consideration and get in touch."

He didn't seem to hear. He stood there as if frozen in thought, and then he tore the check from the book and laid it on the breakfast bar, anchoring it with a spoon. "All you have to do is endorse this check and we have a deal." He spun on his heel, and a moment later the front door banged behind him and flew open again. But Curtis was gone.

"You'd think he'd be a little more careful of the property now that he thinks he owns it," Sam said. He crossed the room to close the door properly.

"Well, it's no thanks to you that he doesn't. Handing him a pen, for heaven's sake—"

"There's no crime in lending the man a pen." He patted his pocket and a look of annoyance crossed his face. "Not returning it, on the other hand...."

"It's not exactly a felony not to give it back—it wasn't a family heirloom fountain pen. Stop changing the subject, Sam. You didn't need to drool all over him."

"I thought you said you were going to put the place up for sale."

"I know," Delainey said slowly. "And you don't need to remind me that I said I'd split the profits with you."

"So why didn't you jump at his offer?"

"Because..." She took a deep breath. "I guess, down deep, I really, really don't want to sell it."

"I noticed that," Sam said dryly. "But do you mean you don't want to sell it to Curtis, or you don't want to sell it at all?"

Delainey frowned. "Look, Sam—I understand why you're upset. If I cashed this check and paid off the mortgage and then split the rest as we agreed, we'd each have more than—"

"Don't say it out loud, honey. I can't bear it. Not unless you're actually going to do it."

"I'm sorry. It would have been easy money, too."

"The easiest I ever earned."

"But I just..." She sighed. "I don't know. I guess I'll have to figure it out for myself before I can explain it to you. And right now, I can't." She stood up and started to clear the dishes.

Sam didn't move. "Do you really believe that things are going to pull through at the bank so you can keep your job?" He sounded almost somber.

Delainey paused as she scraped a plate. "You don't, do you?"

"I don't know. But even if your boss comes back good as new, there's still Jason, and he'll be right there watching you."

Keeping a sharp eye out for any mistake, harboring grudges, whispering behind my back. "You're right," she admitted. "It's not going to be comfortable, working with him."

Sam didn't press the point. He leaned over the breakfast bar, inspecting the check. "Did you see this? It doesn't even have Curtis's name printed on it."

Delainey took a closer look. "It's got a perfectly good account number, though. It's a starter check—when someone first opens an account, it takes a few days to get personalized checks back from the printer. So the bank gives the customer some blanks to use in the meantime."

"So Curtis has just started an account at National City. That ought to be a feather in Jason's cap."

"Nothing like what he's hoping for eventually."

"No, but it's a start. So I'd say that Curtis has presented you with a classic dilemma."

"What do you mean?"

"If you take his offer for the town house, you can get out from under the mortgage and have enough cash left so it doesn't matter—for a while at least—if you lose your job. But if you sell Curtis the town house, he'll be so pleased with you that you could no doubt persuade him to tell Jason to leave you alone. That means you'll probably be able to keep your job. But it also means that you'll need someplace to live, so you should think twice about selling the town house."

"Just what I needed—something else to confuse the situation and make me go 'round and 'round in circles." Delainey started the dishwasher. "I don't want to take his money."

Sam eyed the Christmas tree and started to untangle another set of fairy lights. "Why not? Curtis Whittington's cash will pay off debts and grease the wheels of commerce just the same way as anyone else's would. And he's a free spender, you have to give him that much, Delainey. Offering you three times the price for the town house—the man doesn't stint on the bottom line when he wants something."

"Yeah," Delainey said absently. "He only gets cheap *after* he's bought the company."

Sam paused, apparently studying a knot in the strand of lights. "What's that mean?"

"Nothing much. Just that one of the companies he took over recently seems to have gone from promptly paying their bills to doing so very slowly. That's all." Too late, she caught herself and bit her lip. Sam's question had sounded casual—but was it? And why had she answered it, anyway? What was the matter with her, running off at the mouth like that?

She'd always been scrupulously careful about confidentiality; in fact, her personal code of ethics was more stringent than the bank's written policy. Delainey's own approach was simply not to talk about the bank's customers or their business at all. Of course, she had to admit she'd never had much to worry about in that direction. Her various roommates hadn't shown much interest in the esoteric details of banking, so it wasn't often that she was even tempted to talk about exactly what she did at work, or who she dealt with.

But here she was gossiping with Sam. Sam—who had been curious all along. So curious that it seemed likely he'd deliberately knocked over that stack of files in Josie's office just to see what was inside one or more of them.

Well, she was certain about one thing—whatever Sam might have been looking for in RJ's records, it hadn't been information about George Laurent, because there hadn't been a file with his name on it.

Cut yourself some slack, Delainey. It's been a long day.

Of course she knew, when she stopped to think about it, why her self-imposed censorship had slipped. Between Jason's undermining the deal she'd put together for Elmer Bannister and his refusing to even consider making a loan to George Laurent, her loyalty was wavering.

Definitely time to look for another job, she told herself. "I guess I should grab his offer. It's the best I'm likely to get."

Sam didn't look at her. "All you have to do is endorse the check, he said."

"It's not quite that simple, Sam. It takes a little more paperwork than that. And since I don't actually know where he's staying, that means I can't do anything just now."

"You could look up his address in the bank's computer."

"Do you have any idea how many rules there are against accessing the bank's information for purely personal reasons?"

Sam shrugged. "Then I guess you sleep on it and see how you feel in the morning."

Delainey didn't need to sleep on it. She already knew how she'd feel tomorrow. She'd still be just as reluctant as she was this instant to give up her dream by turning over her beloved town house to Curtis Whittington.

And she'd still be equally convinced that however much she hated the idea, selling it to him was the only decision which made sense.

For a moment, as Sam studied her between the branches of the Christmas tree, Delainey looked like a lost child. She was leaning against the breakfast bar and looking around the room as if she were seeing it for the first time—or the last. The sadness written on her face twisted Sam's heart.

He could almost feel the weight of her regret and the dull ache of her loss. He'd felt them himself.

Then she realized he was watching her, and she pulled herself up straight and smiled. "What are you going to do with your share of the profits, Sam?" Her tone was bright, cheerful. But underneath...

Instead of answering, he put down the still-tangled string of lights and crossed the room to her. "You don't have to be brave every minute, you know."

He half expected that at the first indication of sympathy she'd burst into a flood of tears. But he'd forgotten to take into account that this was Delainey.

Her mouth trembled just a little. That was all, but it was more than Sam could stand. He brushed his fingertip across her lip, trying to still the quivering—and when that didn't work, he tipped her face up and kissed her, slowly and gently.

For an instant she resisted, and then she seemed to melt against him as if she was tired of standing up on her own. She tasted more of loneliness and longing than of passion, though he felt a flicker stir to life, and he knew that now of all times he must keep his head. It would be so easy to take advantage of her right now...

He stopped kissing her, even though it was one of the more difficult things he'd ever done, and buried his face in the glossy golden-brown mass of her hair. The scent of her shampoo tickled his nose, and he forced himself to concentrate on the scent. It was one of those weird herb concoctions that women liked so much. Though it wasn't unpleasant, what was wrong with smelling like something sensible? Roses, maybe, or oranges?

She pulled back just a little, and he let her go. It was, he told himself, the gentlemanly thing to do.

How he wished Emma hadn't taught him to be a gentleman.

*   *   *

Delainey had made up her mind to get it over with as quickly as possible. First thing in the morning, she would find Curtis Whittington and tell him that he'd bought himself a town house. Then she'd rent a place to store her stuff, hire a team of moving men, pay a premium if necessary to get them to shift other jobs to take hers first, and by the end of the day, she and Sam would both be officially homeless.

The only parts of the whole operation that she was looking forward to were cashing Curtis's check and telling Jason he'd have to find another location for his precious office Christmas party.

Maybe Curtis will offer to host it. Sam might even sell him the tree. A predecorated Christmas tree would be right down Curtis's alley.

Things didn't run as smoothly as she'd hoped, however. The first problem she encountered was in finding Curtis, who seemed to have dropped off the face of the earth the minute he'd left the town house the night before.

The first three hotels she checked all denied having any knowledge of him at all. The fourth admitted grudgingly that he had been a guest in the past but refused to tell her when he'd checked out or whether he'd left a forwarding address.

If he did, it was probably my town house, Delainey grumbled, and wished she'd listened last night to Curtis's list of excellent hotels. Though he seemed to her the type who would prefer cookie-cutter corporate chains, she supposed it was possible she was wrong and he'd booked into one of the city's many smaller and more personal hotels. In that case, she could spend all day trying to find him and still be unsuccessful.

Finally, as a last resort, she logged on to the computer system to look up Curtis's new account. She was just starting to type his name into the search field when Jason tapped on her office door and without waiting for an answer came in.

Delainey killed the screen as quickly as she could and turned to face him. "Please knock next time, Jason."

"Why? If you're in the habit of processing loans in your underwear, I'll make sure to pop in at random." He came around her desk and sat on the corner of it, looking down at her. "Or am I more likely to find you satisfying your idle curiosity by browsing through the customers' accounts? That's an offense that could get you fired, Delainey."

"I'm quite aware of that." And there was no doubt in her mind that Jason would consider her looking up Curtis's address as a matter of idle curiosity, not bank business. Fortunately, she hadn't gotten that far, so there was no record for Jason to find, no trail for him to follow. *But I still don't have the damned address, either.* "Frankly, even if I had the inclination to be nosy, I don't have the time. I was just making the point that there's a reason for the door on this office, and I'd appreciate it if you respected it."

Jason shrugged. "What's the big deal? I knocked."

Delainey decided to drop it, because any further discussion would only make him more suspicious. "I'm surprised you and Curtis aren't holed up somewhere cutting the next deal."

"He flew out first thing this morning. Some emergency somewhere."

"You'd think a guy with thousands of employees would have trained some of them so he didn't have to drop everything and run every time a detail comes loose."

"You just can't trust underlings to do things right."

I should remind you of that next time you ask me to spend the weekend crunching numbers. "That's one of the penalties of being the boss, I suppose." She was careful to keep the irony out of her voice. "Having to do the important stuff yourself, I mean. Was there something you wanted, Jason, or did you drop in just to be sociable?''

Jason wanted something, of course. Quite a lot of things. But despite the length of Jason's list, Delainey was conscious of a great sense of relief. As long as Curtis was out of touch, she couldn't do anything about the town house. And the longer Curtis stayed away, the longer her reprieve would be.

When Jason left, leaving the door open behind him, she heard Josie laughing in the outer office, and curiosity drew her to the door to see what was going on. Sam was sitting on the credenza, and on Josie's desk blotter was the biggest box of chocolates that Delainey had ever seen.

Jason paused just long enough to eye both of them skeptically and refuse Josie's offer of a chocolate. As soon as he was gone, Delainey said, ''You two seem to be having a good time.''

Josie turned the chocolate box around to get a better view of the assortment. ''From what Sam's been telling me, it's going to be quite a party.''

''Really? You know, I'm disappointed in you, Josie—letting him buy you off with mere chocolates.''

Sam slid off the credenza and followed Delainey into her office. ''The chocolates were an excuse. I came in to see if I should install that cutting board or take it back to the home supply store and leave the scorch mark for Curtis to deal with.''

''Put it in. Curtis is out of town on business.''

''So we don't need to start packing.''

''Not just yet. What's the matter, Sam? Are you concerned you may have promised too much where this party's concerned? Josie seems to have pretty high hopes for it. Or are you just anxious to be on your way?'' Why hadn't that possibility occurred to her before? ''Where would you go, if we had to leave in a hurry?''

''I'd figure something out.''

"But that's the point. You knew Liz was coming home soon. You must have planned something." How curious, she thought, that she hadn't thought to ask him that until now. "You must have had some idea of where you'd go, what you'd do."

He smiled at her. "Of course I did. But it doesn't matter now, does it?" He kissed the tip of her nose, and was gone.

Delainey lifted a bag of last-minute supplies from the back of her car and paused to sniff the air. The scent of wood smoke was drifting across the lawn—Sam must have started a fire for the party.

He was kneeling in front of the fireplace when she came into the town house. "If you're using the sugar tongs to open the damper," she announced, "let me warn you, I need them for the snack table."

He turned 'round and flourished a wrought-iron poker. "Unlike you, I prefer to use the correct tools for the job. Gran said to tell you she's got appetizers in Liz's oven but she'll come and take over the kitchen as soon as the party starts."

Delainey glanced at the clock and gasped. "That's only half an hour. Where did my afternoon go?" She hurried toward the kitchen to unpack the bag. "Can you help set up the food?"

"When I get the fire going well enough to last a while. It still needs a couple more logs." He went out the patio door.

Delainey was hardly listening because she was running down her to-do list in her head. The relish tray was most critical, she supposed. She grabbed a glass tray—borrowed from Liz's kitchen—and dumped a bag of baby carrots at one end. Celery at the other, olives in the middle—why was it that green olives had to be packed so tightly into the jar? Maybe draining them would help. She tipped the jar over the sink.

Pungent juice cascaded over her hand, stinging the spot where she'd nicked herself with a knife that morning while slicing the celery. She tried to shake the juice off her fingers, and her ring slipped off, hit the bottom of the sink with a clang, and slid down the drain into the garbage disposal as neatly and accurately as a pro golfer's tournament-winning putt.

"Sam!" she called. "I've got a little problem here!"

There was no answer. When she looked around, the fire was blazing nicely but Sam was nowhere to be seen.

"He could have told me he was going to the forest to chop the wood himself," Delainey muttered irritably.

The clock was ticking. It was barely twenty minutes until the party started.

Damn, she thought. Getting a plumber to take the disposal apart would probably cost more than the ring was worth—assuming she could get a plumber at all. She couldn't leave the ring there, either—not only would the guests expect her to be wearing it, but she couldn't exactly put an out-of-order sign on the kitchen sink during a party. The ring might just wash on down the drain without causing any trouble. But she couldn't bet on it. If it didn't slide through, and someone turned on the disposal—well, even a dimestore ring would tear up a disposal in a hurry and leave her with one more thing that needed to be replaced.

No, the ring had to come out. And, now that she thought about it, maybe it would be better if she took care of it herself. Sam hadn't let her forget about her fiasco with the fire yet, so the last thing she wanted to do was hand him another example of basic incompetence.

What was it he'd said about using the correct tool for the job? *Too bad. I'll settle for anything that will do the trick.*

She heard the patio door open at the exact moment she fished the ring out of the depths, and she sighed in relief that she wouldn't have to confess to Sam what she'd done.

But it had been Liz at the door instead. "Emma's first batch of canapés," she announced as she came around the breakfast bar. "Where shall I put these?"

Delainey was rubbing soap into the crevices of the ring. "Are they hot? Set them on the cutting board."

Liz leaned both elbows on the counter. "What are you doing?"

Delainey didn't turn around. "Oh, I dropped the dime-store diamond down the garbage disposal, and now it's coated with slime. This drain must not have been cleaned since it was put in." She reached for a brush. "Maybe I should have just left it there and let it clog up the works. Putting in a new disposal might have been easier than cleaning up the ring."

It was a full fifteen seconds before she realized that Liz hadn't answered. She hadn't moved, either, which made Delainey curious. She looked up to find Liz staring at her, eyes wide.

"What's the matter?" Delainey asked.

"Uh…" Liz gulped. "You didn't stick your hand down there to get it, did you?"

"Of course not. I used my sugar tongs." Delainey pointed at the tongs, still lying beside the sink. "Now I suppose I'll have to sterilize them before I can put them on the table, but—" She inspected the ring. "I wonder if this would turn green if I dunked it in bleach to disinfect it… Oh, what the heck. It's as clean as it's going to get for right now." She slid the ring back onto her finger.

Liz had reached for the tongs. "Is that what this is? Sugar tongs? I got something like it for a wedding gift, but I never knew what to use them for."

"Victorian silver sugar tongs. Used to transport lump sugar from the bowl to the teacup. We're using them to-night for olives, however."

"Oh, that makes sense. I never thought about sugar. I

just knew they were way too small for turning hot dogs on the charcoal grill.''

Delainey blinked. The woman sounded serious. ''Uh…yeah. That would be a pretty good way to burn your hand. The intense heat of the grill wouldn't be too good for the silver, either.''

''Really? You see,'' Liz confided, ''Jack's the one with all the culture. I have no idea about this stuff.''

Delainey hesitated. There was something about the look on Liz's gamine face… ''You're missing him, aren't you?''

Liz shook her head, almost defiantly. Then, very softly, she said, ''Yeah.''

''So call him.''

''I can't.''

''Why not? They have phones on cruise ships, don't they?''

Liz was looking down at her hands. Delainey wondered if she was looking at the marquise diamond, or her wedding ring, or seeing something else altogether. ''Because he's the one who started it.''

''It doesn't matter who started it, Liz. What counts is that somebody is big enough to swallow their pride and stop it before it's too late.'' Delainey started cleaning the sugar tongs.

The stereo system came to life with a blast of Christmas carols that hurt Delainey's ears. The volume dropped to a soft murmur, and a moment later Sam came around the breakfast bar into the kitchen. ''Ah,'' he said. ''Scrubbing the poker like a good little housewife, I see.''

Liz looked at him as if he'd slipped a cog. ''I'd better go get the next batch of appetizers, or Emma will be ready to broil me instead of the mini-pizzas.''

''Five minutes to go,'' Sam said.

Delainey dropped the tongs. Five minutes, and most of her list yet to do…

He gave her a curious look. "Are you always this nervous before you give a party?"

"Compared to this," Delainey said, "I've never given a party."

The doorbell rang. "I think that means it's too late to back out now," Sam said, and went to answer it.

Josie and her husband and a couple of the other secretaries breezed in, followed by one of Delainey's fellow loan officers. Before long the living room was full and the party had spilled over into the kitchen, where Emma was holding court and pressing people into service, and even upstairs. Delainey hoped Sam had remembered to put the sheets and pillows from the futon into the farthest, darkest corner of the linen closet so no one would wonder why they had extras lying around.

She didn't know when Jason arrived; she first glimpsed him in the corner between the fireplace and the patio door, with a glass in his hand, talking to Emma. Alarm bells went off in her head. How—and why—had he lured Emma out of the kitchen? Was he asking about Delainey and Sam? And if so, what was Emma likely to say?

She was intercepted twice before she could get across the room, and when she finally reached Emma's side, the woman was talking to Jason about something that sounded very much like Delainey's business incubator. "I think it's a marvelous idea," Emma was saying.

Jason rolled his eyes at Delainey and reached for her elbow. "Yes, yes," he said to Emma. "You'll excuse me now, though—I want another drink and I must talk to my hostess about this lovely party." He drew Delainey away and demanded, "What are you trying to accomplish? I'm warning you, setting up a crazy old witch to tell me you have great ideas is not going to cut it."

"She's not crazy, she's not a witch, and I didn't set up anything."

"Sure." He moved off toward the makeshift bar.

"That's what's wrong with the whole idea, you know," he called over his shoulder. "It encourages tabbies like that to think they're entrepreneurs."

Sam must have told Emma about the incubator idea, Delainey thought. It was too bad he hadn't also warned her to steer clear of Jason.

At least the confrontation had taken her mind off her nerves. She was actually starting to enjoy the party.

The front door opened again, and Delainey looked up automatically to greet the newcomer. But her smile froze when she saw who it was. "This is an employee party," she said to no one in particular. "What's Curtis Whittington doing here?"

Jason came up beside her, swirling a fresh glass. "Interesting you should ask. I don't suppose there's any point in trying to keep it under wraps anymore. The board of directors will meet on Monday afternoon to make the deal official." He grinned at Delainey. "What deal, you ask? It's just a simple thing, really. He's buying the bank."

CHAPTER NINE

IF JASON had picked up Sam's new wrought-iron poker and slammed it across her head, Delainey couldn't have been more stunned. Curtis Whittington was buying out National City?

That does it, then.

It was only now, however, when Jason had ripped away her illusions as harshly as tearing a bandage from a wound, that Delainey began to realize the self-deceptive game she'd been playing. Until that moment, she had still been comforting herself with the thought that everything would be all right when RJ came back.

She had believed she was facing the truth—and to an extent, she had. She'd agreed with Sam that continuing to work with Jason, even if RJ was in charge, would be difficult. She'd taken the first steps toward selling the town house.

But underneath, she'd still been clinging to her security blanket. *When RJ came back, it would be all right.*

Now, if Curtis Whittington bought the bank, nothing would ever be right again at National City. Not for Delainey, at least.

She could see the plan rolling out in front of her. RJ would be forced into retirement, if he didn't go voluntarily. Jason would be at the head of the business loan division... Unless, of course, he moved even further upward in the hierarchy. Jason probably pictured himself as bank president—and why not? As Curtis's right-hand man, controlling the finances, he could probably call himself whatever he wanted.

But there would be no place in such an organization for Delainey. It was time to face the facts, and to act.

Sam came up beside her. "Delainey, did you see who just came in?"

She was having trouble focusing. "Curtis is buying the bank."

"It was my idea, of course," Jason said proudly. "A perfectly natural plan, too. Why borrow money from someone else when you can loan it to yourself?"

Sam appeared to be giving the rhetorical question serious thought. "But if a person has that much cash in the first place, why does he need a bank?"

Jason laughed derisively. "Well, it's obvious you don't know much about big business. Aren't you at least going to welcome your guest, Delainey?"

He didn't wait for an answer, but strolled across to the door to greet Curtis.

Sam said, "Are you all right?"

"Curtis is buying the bank," she repeated. She hardly recognized her own voice.

"Yes, I figured that out," Sam said dryly. "It's a good thing you put that check safely away before the party."

"What check?"

"The check for the town house. You did put it away, didn't you, Delainey? It's not still sitting on the breakfast bar with the phone book and the electric bill?"

The town house.

Do it right now, she told herself, *while you're still numb. It won't hurt as much that way.* And she'd have to do it quickly, before Curtis figured out that he could buy it for a whole lot less if waited till next week—after Jason fired her.

But she didn't move. She looked helplessly up at Sam, and suddenly, with an impact so brutal it made Jason's announcement seem pleasant, she understood why she was hesitating. Why she'd been playing the soothing game all week.

For days, she'd been telling herself that things would work out, that she could keep her job, that she wouldn't have to sell the town house after all. And at first it had been the job and the town house that truly mattered. They would always matter, of course—the career she had worked so hard to build, and her first real home, the symbol of her dreams.

But somewhere along the way the job and the town house had faded into the background, until now it wasn't their own value that was most important. It wasn't even the hard work or the dreams that they represented. They had gotten all mixed up in her mind with something else. With Sam.

And now she knew it was Sam that counted. Only Sam.

As long as she had the job and the town house, she needed Sam. She needed him to play the adoring fiancé, and she needed him to get the house in condition to sell.

But once the job and the town house were gone, she would no longer have an excuse for keeping Sam beside her. And once she didn't need a fiancé and a handyman— once he'd collected his share of the profits from the sale of the town house—his reasons for staying with her vanished as well.

That was why she had been pretending all week that when everything had finally settled out, she'd still have her job, and she'd still have her town house. Because that meant she'd still have Sam, too.

And Sam was what she wanted. He was everything she wanted. Somewhere along the way, in the midst of the games, the pretending had become real. She had fallen in love with Sam Wagner.

"Delainey?" he said. "You do remember the whole idea of selling the town house—don't you?"

She blinked and tried to pull herself back. The party,

right—she was surrounded by a party...and there was something she had to do right now....

She swallowed hard. "I don't want to, Sam."

She would have gone on, but the few words seemed to have taken all the strength and breath she had. Her voice had scarcely been audible, even to her own ears.

Sam's jaw tightened, and his eyes turned icy blue. "I see," he said levelly. "It's your choice to make, of course." He turned on his heel and plunged into the crowd.

Delainey stared after him. Why hadn't he let her explain? She could have told him...

Told him what? That she loved him?

Oh, that would have gone over well. *I don't want to sell the town house because I want us to live together in it forever and ever.*

No, she told herself. She was glad he hadn't waited around and let her fall all over herself to tell him what an idiot she was about him. Especially not when she knew perfectly well why he was so irritated. What was it Sam had said about his share of the profits from the town house? *The easiest money I ever earned,* that was it. No wonder he was put out with her for changing her mind again.

And if she had told him why she didn't want to sell— and he'd looked at her with contempt... She shuddered at the idea. No, it was much better this way. *Skip the explanation, just do what you have to do.*

But while she'd been standing there trying to absorb the dual blows of the bank sale and her new self-knowledge, Curtis had disappeared.

Delainey looked all over the town house, but neither he nor Jason was to be found. Josie saw her searching and told her that they'd gone.

"They probably went looking for more excitement," the secretary said. "But I think it's a better party without them. Let's turn up the music and dance!"

*   *   *

The town house was a shambles after the party. Though there was no actual damage, used glasses, paper plates, crumpled napkins, and bits of food lurked in the most unexpected of pleasures, and it took Delainey most of the day on Sunday to get it straightened up.

Worse than the mess, however, was the fact that the check Curtis had given her to pay for the town house was nowhere to be found.

She was almost certain she'd last seen it propped up on the breakfast bar between the salt shaker and a mug full of odds and ends. But it certainly wasn't there now.

Had she put it away when she was cleaning up before the party, in such a frenzy that she didn't even remember doing it?

Had it gotten in with the newspapers and been tossed out accidentally?

Or had one of the party guests seen it and gotten sticky fingers?

She couldn't believe it of any of her guests—her co-workers. And yet there it was. Unless she found the slip of paper, she couldn't help but be just a little suspicious.

She mentioned it to Sam on Monday morning, breaking the silence in which she'd sipped her coffee.

"What does it matter?" he said. "It's made out to you. Nobody else could do anything with it."

"Oh, really? Someday I'll tell you some horror tales about the banking business." Her heart twisted painfully as she realized how casually the words had slipped from her. *Someday.* But that day wouldn't ever come for them. Her voice grew a little sharper. "I'd just like to know where it is, all right? I'd rather it not turn up in Jason's hands, for instance."

"Since I don't have anything better to do today, I'll turn the place upside down." He was still sitting at the breakfast bar, both hands cupped around his coffee mug, when she left.

Why do I even care? Delainey asked herself. It wasn't as if she didn't have enough troubles already. Her job was hanging by a single thread, and Jason was standing by with a pair of scissors at the ready. She was the owner of a six-figure check that would pay off her mortgage and take a great deal of pain out of the next few months of joblessness, but she couldn't lay her hands on it at the moment, much less actually turn it into cash.

But instead, she was breaking her heart over Sam. Sam, who'd been sitting in the kitchen in jeans, barefoot, his hair rumpled, with nothing planned for his day. Sam, who'd been out of a job and without a home for—she realized she didn't even know how long. Sam, who showed no interest in a business opportunity or in going back to school...

Sam, who had held her, soothed her, empathized when she was down and challenged her when she was feeling sorry for herself. Sam, who in just a few days had turned almost every square inch of the town house sparkling white, arranged a party, set up a Christmas tree, greeted her each evening with a hot meal and a smile. Sam, who had tenderly massaged her scalp until she'd practically been jelly in his hands.

Sam, who could have taken her to bed just about anytime in the last week, but hadn't.

Why not? Because despite the repartee, he wasn't interested? Or because he didn't want the complications?

Remembering the way he'd kissed her, she was pretty certain it wasn't a lack of interest. Not that his reason made much difference in how Delainey felt. As far as she was concerned, the difference between being thought of as undesirable or just plain troublesome was pretty much just a flip of the coin. It would be better just not to think about it at all.

But whenever she tried not to think of Sam, she came squarely back to the problem of Curtis and the check. Sooner or later she was going to have to face Curtis and confess. Since she'd rather do that in person, she figured her best chance would be to catch him right before the board of directors met that afternoon. With any luck he'd have his mind on the bank instead of the town house and he'd write her a replacement check without a second thought.

The moment Delainey arrived at the bank, however, she took the head teller aside. "There's a check I want you to watch for," she said. "It's made out to me, written on a brand-new account. And I've lost it."

The teller didn't even wince. "You think someone will try to cash it?"

"Not really," Delainey said. "I probably stuck it in a drawer, or in the linen closet, or in the sugar bowl, when I had something else on my mind. But it disappeared over the weekend. So if someone actually did steal it, they're likely to try cashing it today, thinking I might not have noticed it was gone."

"You could call the account-holder and ask if they want to put a stop-payment order on it."

Delainey shook her head. "I'd rather not, Sally. I really don't think it'll show up at all, but it's only reasonable to take a few precautions."

"Stopping payment would be a lot safer. The odds of a check coming back here to be cashed are pretty small, especially if whoever's trying to pull off the scam knows anything about banking."

That's a safe bet, Delainey thought. *Because that description covers everybody at the party except Emma and Sam and Liz.*

"And even if they brought it here, we could miss it," the teller warned. She shook her head. "Watching for one single check out of the thousands we process every day—"

"It's not just an ordinary check," Delainey admitted. "It's a big enough amount that if anybody tries to cash it at any bank, we'll get a call for verification."

The head teller raised her eyebrows. "You want to tell me exactly how big this check is?"

Delainey swallowed hard and told her.

"And you *lost* it? Or you think that whoever took it believes you might not have even noticed that it's missing? How on earth anyone could overlook that kind of money—"

"You deal with those sorts of numbers every day."

"Yes—but not with my own personal name attached to them. Never mind. I don't want to know how it happened. I'll let you know if I hear anything."

"Thanks, Sally."

"But I still think you should get the payment stopped instead."

Delainey didn't tell her that was the last thing she wanted to do. She didn't want Curtis's check to be rendered worthless—because if she did get her hands on it again before she came face-to-face with the merger king, Delainey was going to cash it herself just as fast as a teller could count out the bills.

Knowing she'd done everything she could for the moment, Delainey went on to her office, glanced at the printed schedule Josie handed her, closed her door and began phoning every contact she'd ever made in the banking business in the whole city.

If this was going to be her last day at National City, as it seemed it might be, then she was determined to spend it doing her job. Which in this case was to find George Laurent the financing he needed to keep his packaging-supplies business afloat—even if the money didn't come from National City.

It was almost lunchtime and she was checking off the fifth name on her list when Josie opened her office door. "Ms. Hodges, Sally's on the phone. Something about a check."

Sally, the head teller. Delainey stared at the phone for a

moment, feeling befuddled, before she picked it up. Even though she'd set up the trap herself, she'd had no expectation that it would actually catch someone. She'd believed that Curtis's check must be lurking in some dark corner of the town house—perfectly safe, just temporarily unaccounted for.

But this meant that someone *had* stolen it. Someone who had been at her party.

She picked up the phone. "Sally? What have you heard?"

"That check you wanted us to watch for. It's here right now."

"*Here?* You mean right here in the building?"

"At window three. The teller's stalling."

"I'll be right out." She broke the connection just as Sally started to say something else, and hurried down the hall.

The lobby was always busy on Mondays, when customers came in to transact business that had built up over the weekend. All of the teller windows were open and occupied, and there was a line of customers stretching halfway back to the main door and blocking her view of window three. All she could see was the back view of a tall man with dark hair...

She felt as if she'd been slugged. "No," she said. "No. Not Sam."

It wasn't possible. And yet there he was, right before her eyes.

She made her way slowly through the crowd and stepped up beside him at the window. "Well, hello, Sam."

The young teller gave a little sigh of relief, and from just behind the teller's chair, Sally murmured, "Take a break, Alison. I'll handle things here for a few minutes."

Delainey didn't look at the head teller. She knew the sympathetic look she'd meet would be more than she could stand right now. So she put her chin up and stared at Sam. "I see you found the check."

To his credit, Sam didn't deny it. He didn't even flinch. He turned to face her, propping an elbow on the marble counter. "It was in a kitchen cabinet, under a coffee mug. Gran must have put it there to keep it safe."

"Yeah," Delainey muttered. "I can just see Emma doing that... So if it was safe in the cabinet, what's it doing here—attached to your hand? No, don't tell me. Let me think. You must have been bringing it to me."

"Actually, that's exactly what I was doing."

"Right. Tell me another fairy tale. You knew perfectly well you wouldn't find me sitting at a teller window, so why are you standing in front of one? Asking directions?"

"I was just checking on something on my way to your office." He looked over his shoulder. "Speaking of your office, can we talk about this in private? People are waiting, and..."

There was a murmur of agreement from the line.

"Excellent idea." She took the check out of his hand "I'll just keep hold of this to make sure it's safely transported."

Josie greeted them with a smile. "Hi, Sam. That was a great party, you know—you were right. I really had a—"

Delainey whisked Sam past before Josie could finish her sentence. She shut the door and leaned against it because her knees were feeling weak, too unsteady to allow her to walk across the room just yet. "What were you doing, Sam? Trying to cash it so you could get your share of the profits after all? Or were you planning to keep the whole thing?"

"Ask the teller. She'll tell you I never said anything about cashing it." His tone was calm.

"That doesn't prove that you weren't going to try. You know, I was just wondering as I walked down the hall what kind of idiot would try to cash that check right here, directly under my nose. But now it all makes sense. You couldn't cash it anywhere else because there would be too many questions. But here, where everybody knows you're my fiancé, you stood a chance of pulling it off. If you told them you were doing it for me—''

''I wasn't trying to cash it, Delainey. I wanted information, and I got it. You might find it interesting to know what I found out.''

She was curious, and angry at herself for even wanting to listen. But at least her knees weren't weak anymore. She walked across to her desk. ''Sure, tell me.''

''The account that check is written on doesn't contain enough money to cover it.''

Delainey sat down with a thump. ''You managed to charm the teller into letting you know how much is in the account?''

''I don't know exactly what the balance is—so don't fire her for spilling classified information, because she didn't. But I do know that piece of paper you're holding is worthless.''

''They must have told you that as a reason to delay you long enough for me to get there. That's all.''

Sam shook his head. ''It wasn't a stall tactic. The teller isn't a good enough actress to pull off that kind of act. She was shocked.''

Delainey frowned. ''Inadequate funds? It can't be. It was only opened last week and the initial deposit was five million.'' Too late, she bit her tongue. That was exactly the sort of information that bank employees weren't supposed to share—the very sort she'd been ready to scold the teller for letting slip.

Sam had caught her gaffe, that was clear from the sparkle in his eyes. But instead of rubbing it in, he said, ''Maybe Curtis spent it already. At the rate he goes around writing checks, it wouldn't take a week to run through five million.''

"I'm betting it's right there where it's supposed to be and the teller is a better actress than you think."

"Well, there's one way to find out who's right." He pointed at her laptop computer.

Delainey wheeled her chair around and logged on to the network. It took a few seconds for the search to find Curtis's name.

Sam seemed in no hurry. He sat down, reached for a handful of paper clips, and started to make a chain.

"Nervous?" Delainey asked. The screen flickered, the account record came up, and she couldn't suppress a gasp.

"Let me guess," Sam said. "He's got twenty-seven dollars to his name."

"Sixty-three," Delainey admitted. "There has to be a mistake. Maybe the deposit hasn't been credited."

"In a week? Give me a break."

"It happens. With that big a deposit—especially with a new customer—it's prudent to make sure the check is real before you make the funds available."

"One of the favorite new scams," Sam said. "Make a fancy-looking check on your home computer, use it to start a new account, then take the money out before the bank discovers that the check you deposited was a work of art instead of finance. But in that case, where did the sixty-three dollars come from?"

Delainey wasn't listening. "Jason's going to have a fit if that's what's happened—somebody holding back Curtis Whittington's funds till the check cleared." She pushed another button and the history of the account came up. For a moment, as numbers scrolled on and off the screen, she thought the computer must have hit a glitch. There couldn't have been this much activity in a week. But still the numbers rolled past.

The initial deposit had been credited, there was no doubt about that. So had a dozen others, and more than a hundred withdrawals. Delainey added it up in her head. In exactly a week, Curtis had run more than fifteen million dollars through his account.

Sam sat up straighter. "What's the matter?"

She ignored him and started looking at each individual transaction, pulling up the scanned image of the checks that had been deposited and those that had been written on the account. "This doesn't make any sense. The money comes in from a holding company overseas, and it goes back out—sometimes to the same holding company, sometimes to a different one, but most often to one of his corporations. There's only one missing check number—the one he wrote to me—because it hasn't been cashed yet. A good deal of this money is just going in circles. In fact, I wouldn't be surprised if it's the same money."

Sam came around the desk. "What does that mean?"

"He's churning the account. Making it look like there's more money than there actually is. If you run five million dollars through an account three times—depositing it, writing a check to yourself, depositing it again—you look like a fifteen-million dollar customer."

"Anything illegal about that?" Sam's tone was crisp.

Delainey shook her head. "I just can't imagine why he'd bother. Hey, you're not supposed to see all this." She put a hand over the screen.

"Didn't see a thing," Sam said. "Look, dear, I'd love to stick around, shoot the breeze, take you to lunch, but—"

He was on his way to the door when she remembered Curtis's check. "Hey, what about this?" She waved it at him. "You still haven't explained what you were doing with it."

Sam came back to the desk. He took the check out of her hand, laid it on the blotter, and planted a fingertip on the note Curtis had scrawled in the memo section of the check. "See this?"

"Yeah. So what? It says the check is to pay for the town house."

"No. It says that endorsing the check transfers owner-ship. If you'd signed your name on the back of this check, Curtis would own a town house—even if the check was no good."

Delainey felt as if she'd been hit by a truck. Then sanity reasserted itself. "That would never stand up in court."

"When I talked to Jack this morning, he thought it was a very gray area."

"You called him on the cruise ship? Never mind. Attorneys think everything's a gray area."

"That's my point. Do you really want to fight Curtis Whittington's entire team of lawyers over it?" He reached across the desk to flick a fingertip along her cheekbone. "You can thank me later."

A moment later he was gone.

By early afternoon, Delainey had found a banker sympa-thetic to George Laurent's cause. She called him at the packaging firm to ask if she could send his application to her colleague.

He hesitated. "I'd rather deal with you, Ms. Hodges. I like your style."

"I'd rather do it that way too," Delainey said. "But this will be better for you. It's a good package, and a lower interest rate than I could offer you." *If I could get you anything at all.*

She was still thinking about Curtis Whittington, however, and the sly way he'd made his pitch to buy the town house. The longer she thought about how he'd behaved that eve-ning, the more she wondered if Sam was right after all.

Curtis had offered a price generous enough to tempt a saint and he'd written a check on the spot. And—perhaps more important—he'd asked for immediate possession. If she had taken the check that night and left him there in the town house... *All you have to do is endorse this check and we have a deal,* he'd said that evening.

Well, Sam was definitely right about one thing: lawyers could argue for years over whether that was really a binding contract.

Curtis had been counting on her to be greedy. And she had to admit that if it hadn't been for Sam, she might have fallen into the trap. But it hadn't been Sam's action this morning in checking out the state of Curtis's bank account that had saved her. It was Sam himself. She'd hesitated because she wanted the town house to be home for both of them.

You can thank me later, he'd said. She would, no doubt. But she would never, never tell him what she was really thanking him for.

The whole thing still made no sense, though. Why would Curtis Whittington try to scam her out of her town house? As a game? A challenge? A way to get even with her for rejecting his advances the night they'd met?

That felt more likely. Because surely a man with that much money didn't care how much he paid for a town house…

Something Sam had said at the party came back to her. She'd hardly heard it at the time, because she'd been in such a state of shock over Jason's announcement. But now it echoed in her head.

"If a person has that much cash in the first place, why does he need a bank?"

And suddenly it all fell into place in her head. The massive amounts of deposits and withdrawals in Curtis's account made sense now. He wasn't churning money, depositing the same five million over and over in order to make himself look like a more important customer.

He was laundering it.

He was taking money from some shady—possibly criminal—enterprise and running it through holding companies, corporations, and bank accounts until the most meticulous accountant would have trouble tracking where it had come from or what path it had taken.

George Laurent had been dead on target when he'd said Curtis Whittington's operation bore more resemblance to the Mafia than to a business. But even George hadn't meant it literally.

Who would suspect the merger king, with his legitimate operations spread across the country, to be dealing with illegal cash on the side?

And if he could do that with just a regular account, what was he going to be able to pull off if he managed to buy the bank?

Delainey couldn't prove it, of course. Even though she knew it as well as she knew her own name, there was not a single thing she could do about it. The board was already gathering for their scheduled meeting; there was no time for investigation.

But surely just the whisper of controversy would be enough to bring the deal to a halt. The success of Curtis's scheme rested on the fact that no one suspected him. So if someone started asking uncomfortable questions...

That someone would have to be Delainey. There was no one else.

The conference room was buzzing with conversation as the members of the board milled around, coffee and sodas in hand, waiting for the meeting to begin. Delainey stopped just inside the door to look over the group. Who would be most likely to listen?

The crowd shifted and with a flood of relief she saw RJ. He was already seated near the head of the table, looking weak but with more color in his face than when she'd last seen him, still in the hospital. RJ was the answer; he would listen to her, as he always had.

She started toward him.

Jason blocked her path. "Don't go upsetting RJ with this prejudice of yours, Delainey."

For an instant she wondered if he had read her mind.

RJ leaned to one side to look around Jason. "What brings you into the board meeting, Delainey?"

Jason kept step with her. "She's got this personal dislike for Curtis, RJ. Nothing you need to listen to."

"I have some information you need to hear before the board makes a decision, RJ. Curtis isn't what he seems. He's—"

"She came on to him and he wasn't interested," Jason said loudly. "So now she's trying anything she can to get even."

RJ frowned. "That doesn't sound like you, Delainey."

"I've discovered something you need to take a look at, RJ. Curtis's new account here at the bank shows a lot of very strange transactions in a short period of time, and—"

"And exactly what," Jason said, "was your reason for inspecting the activity in Curtis's account? Or did you have a reason at all, beyond personal curiosity? And does this accusation have anything to do with the little flap this morning in the lobby—something about a check that had been stolen from you?"

Delainey bit her lip. If there had been a little more time, she thought. If she'd had a chance to prepare, to dig a little deeper... But as it was, she had nothing solid to show RJ. She had only her power of persuasion. And now Jason had so efficiently undermined her that there was no point in even going on.

Still, she had to try. If she could make just one person curious enough to ask questions...

"RJ," she pleaded, "if you'll just look at the account—"

Jason studied his nails. "Your time might be better spent, RJ, in asking Ms. Hodges why she's been arranging for our customers to get loans from other banks instead of from us."

The accusation almost knocked Delainey off her feet. How could Jason possibly know about that?

He smiled at her and answered the unspoken question. "I got a call from George Laurent a little while ago, telling me what a wonderful person you are to arrange everything for him—not only getting him a loan, but at a lower rate of interest. From one of our competitors."

Poor George—he thought he was doing me a favor by complimenting me to my boss.

RJ's voice was as strong as ever, and more stern than Delainey had ever heard before. "Is this true, Delainey?"

"Yes, sir. But—"

"I don't wish to hear excuses. You're terminated immediately, and I want you out of the building before this board meeting is over."

Jason had moved around behind RJ. Probably, Delainey thought, because he didn't want the boss to catch him smirking at her.

The door opened just as Delainey turned to go out, and Sam breezed into the room with the same easy confidence as if he was stepping onto the squash court.

For a few seconds Delainey thought she was hallucinating, particularly because this was a Sam she'd never seen before. He was carrying a calfskin briefcase, and he was wearing a navy pin-striped suit with a white shirt...

He does own a tie, she thought absently. *Unless he only borrowed it.*

"Ladies and gentlemen," Sam said, and his voice cut across the conversation in the room as effectively as if he'd shouted. "Please take your seats so we can start. I'm going to pass out materials while you're getting settled." He moved briskly to the head of the table, excused himself and stepped past the board member who was standing there, and set his briefcase down next to the lectern. With an easy economy of motion he opened the case, took out a stack of documents, and began to pass them down the length of the table.

Delainey could feel the blood pounding in her ears.

Desperately, she tried to make sense of what she was seeing, but nothing clicked. Why was he here? What was his connection with this deal? He wasn't part of the bank, or surely she would have known it. She didn't know every last employee, but someone who pulled off this sort of deal—she'd have heard the name, at least. But he wasn't part of Curtis's team, either. If he had been, he would already have known all about the man—or else he wouldn't have wanted to know any more than he had to.

Lawyer? Accountant? The go-between who'd arranged the takeover of the bank?

One thing was coming clear, though. Whatever Sam might be, he wasn't what she'd thought. He wasn't anything like the man he'd let her believe in.

"Who *are* you?" she said.

Her voice was little more than a whisper, but in the suddenly quiet room, it carried from near the foot of the table, where she was standing, all the way to Sam.

He met her gaze across the room, and she could see regret in his eyes. But regret for what? Something he'd done? Or something he was about to do?

"Until six months ago," Sam said, "when Curtis Whittington took it over, I was one of the owners of Foursquare Electronics. For the last half year, I've been an unemployed electrical engineer killing time until the terms of the takeover allowed me go to back to work. And now—thanks to you, Delainey—I'm the man with the proof that Curtis Whittington is a crook."

She could hardly take it in.

Memories were flashing through her mind like electrical shocks. Sam, wiring up the outlet in her kitchen, eyeing Curtis's photo on the magazines she'd brought home, and asking if she was a fan of the merger king. Sam, turning up at the table next to hers at the mansion on the night she had dinner with Curtis and Jason, when she'd thought he was just entertaining himself by causing trouble. Sam, using her check to find everything he could about Curtis Whittington…

No wonder he'd been so cooperative. No wonder he'd played along with the farce of being her fiancé.

He'd been using her every step of the way.

CHAPTER TEN

THE conference room broke into a cacophony as the board realized what was happening. Voices collided and rose in frustration, anger, and confusion.

Delainey leaned against the nearest wall, letting the noise flow over her, making no effort to distinguish one voice from another. Everyone seemed to be talking at once.

Except for Curtis, who sat silent near the head of the table, only a few seats away from Sam. He was one of the few in the room who hadn't jumped up at Sam's announcement; he sat perfectly still, arms folded across his chest.

Sam stood at the head of the table with one hand braced on the lectern and waited.

The board member in the seat nearest where Delainey was standing was an older woman. She flipped open the packet of documents which had just been passed to her, pulled a pair of reading glasses up from the chain around her neck where they'd been dangling, and began to read. Her silence seemed to spread, and gradually the noise level in the room dropped. When it was finally quiet, Sam began to talk.

Delainey was still too stunned to take in everything he said or to judge the evidence he presented. All she heard was the measured cadence of his voice as he laid out the facts.

It was a familiar voice—oh, so achingly familiar—and yet it was also completely alien. For this wasn't Sam chatting, teasing, even arguing. This was a Sam she'd never heard before, a man who was obviously used to laying out facts and giving orders.

She knew he talked about the holding companies where

Curtis's money had come from, and where it had gone—
holding companies whose names he had seen over her
shoulder, on her computer screen. He laid out in detail what
business they were really in, who their clients were, how
Curtis's connections with them had grown. And he talked
about how Curtis used his legitimate businesses—ones like
Foursquare Electronics—to conceal his other activities.

"The merger king selected a business to acquire not because of the product, or the patents, or the customer list, or
the manufacturing line," Sam said. "He didn't care what
kind of business it was, as long as it generated revenue
which he could inflate with laundered money. Every company Curtis Whittington has acquired has become just a
little more successful, a little more profitable, than anyone
would have expected."

Delainey remembered that one of the magazine profiles
she'd read had called it Curtis Whittington's magic touch.

"The high profit margins he reported raised the stock
price, and then he used the stock to acquire the next company. He didn't run enough money through any one company to raise suspicions about why it was suddenly looking
like a gold mine. Instead, he'd just go buy another one and
start again."

There were interruptions and questions from the board,
tangents and sidelines and distractions, until Delainey's
head was aching as she tried to keep it all straight. But at
least, she reflected, the bank was safe. The board would
never vote to go along with the sale as long as there were
questions of this magnitude. And that was all she'd really
hoped to do in the first place—to keep the bank safe. She
could go now.

Suddenly she remembered that RJ had told her to be out
of the building before the meeting was over.

Funny, she thought. *I'd almost forgotten that in the middle of all that, I lost my job.*

She wondered idly if RJ would apologize and offer to

hire her back, or if he'd stand by Jason. Not that it mattered much to her at the moment. Right now, she just wanted to get away.

She asked Josie to bring her a box and some newspapers and went on into her office to begin stripping it of her personal items. She was taking the framed diploma down off the wall above her desk when the door opened and Josie came in with the packing materials.

The secretary stopped dead just inside the room. "What are you doing?" she screeched. "You can't leave. You're the best boss I've ever had!"

"Sorry," Delainey said. "It's not up to me."

A squeak from the still-open door drew her attention, and RJ's secretary wheeled his chair in. RJ held up a hand. "Let's not be hasty about this, Delainey."

Delainey folded the diploma into a newspaper and set it in the box. "I'm just following your orders."

"I meant, of course, that I was the one who perhaps was hasty. Let's stop right here and talk about this."

"You can talk if you want, RJ. I'll listen."

She had never known the old man could be so eloquent, and if she hadn't been too numb to feel, he might have been successful in convincing her. As it was, she let him go on for a while, until she realized that the healthy color she'd noticed when she first saw him in the conference room had drained away. He looked gray, and old, and ill.

"Stop it, RJ," she told him. "You'll put yourself in the hospital again if you're not careful."

"I'm not leaving till you tell me you're back on the team."

"The team," Delainey mused. "Oh, yes, the all-important team."

Over his shoulder she saw a flicker of movement. Sam was standing in Josie's office, just outside Delainey's door. She wondered how long he'd been there.

"Go home, RJ," she said. "Don't worry about it any more. Just go home and rest."

He seized her hand between his. "That's great, Delainey."

As the secretary turned RJ's chair around, Delainey noticed that Sam had gone as well.

Two down, she thought. *I'm doing better than I'd expected.*

RJ said over his shoulder, "See you tomorrow, Delainey."

She couldn't lie to him. "I don't know whether I'll be here. I have a lot of things to think about."

"You go home and think about everything you've invested in this bank in the last ten years, and I'm confident you'll be back to work tomorrow, my dear. We'll talk about it more then. If you want more responsibility, a bigger title..."

She shook her head. When he was gone, she stopped packing and sat down at her desk, and stared at nothing for a while.

The town house felt cold, though the furnace was running when Delainey came in. But of course it wasn't heated air which was missing. It was Sam's warmth, reflected in the shared cup of coffee, the chat over dinner, the glow of the Christmas tree lights.

Wherever he'd gone when he left the bank, it hadn't been back to the town house. At least, he hadn't packed up his belongings. His pocketknife and a handful of coins still lay on the breakfast bar. She picked up the knife and turned it slowly over and over in her hand.

She'd misjudged him from the start, when she'd assumed he was unemployed because he didn't want to bother to seek work, living with his grandmother because it was convenient. Why hadn't she caught on?

And—perhaps more importantly—why hadn't he corrected her?

That one had an obvious answer. Very obvious, in fact, though it was less than pleasant to face. *Because it didn't matter to him what I thought.*

And, of course, because she could be useful to him. So he'd deliberately kept her in the dark....

She looked at the stark white heart which still stood out against the original beige square, right above the mantel. How many times had he refused to paint over their linked initials? *I can't bring myself to do it—you'll have to.* How touching and sentimental—and completely bogus.

Liz tapped at the patio door, and Delainey went to open it. "Hi," Liz said. "I saw you come home and wondered if you'd like to have dinner with me at the Mansion tonight. You and Sam, of course."

You and Sam. So casual, so easy, so natural-sounding. So impossible.

Delainey shook her head.

"Bad day at the office?"

The casual question was an understatement of such magnificent proportions that Delainey started to laugh—only then she couldn't stop. "I know it shouldn't matter," she gasped finally. "It's such a little thing, compared to everything else that's happened today. But Sam and I are through."

Liz frowned. "The engagement? But—"

"I know," Delainey said. "What's the big deal about breaking an engagement that was a farce from the beginning? But—" She turned her hand to look one last time at the ring she was still wearing, then pulled it off her finger and held it up so the center stone caught the light, and remembered the way Liz had looked at her the day Delainey had dropped it down the disposal. "This isn't just a dimestore diamond, is it? It's real."

"Yeah," Liz admitted. "But I don't know why he didn't want you to find out."

"I know why." *Because I would ask too many questions about why a guy without a job or a place to live had a diamond ring knocking around in his pocket.*

And come to think of it, why did he have it? It certainly wasn't a collector's item, and it didn't seem old enough to be a family heirloom.

"Who did he buy it for, Liz?"

Liz bit her lip. "Me."

Delainey didn't even blink. After so many shocks, one atop the other, the new ones seemed to be losing their impact. "You and Sam were engaged?"

"Not for very long. I always liked that ring, though. I picked it out."

Now it made sense. Liz was a dear, but a woman who could contemplate using a set of silver tongs to turn hot dogs on a barbecue grill certainly would choose the showiest ring in the case, no matter what else was offered. That was simply Liz's style.

"I'm surprised he didn't let you keep it," Delainey mused.

"He would have. But Jack…well, Jack didn't think it was a good idea for me to have it."

So Sam had kept it instead. For sentimental value, obviously.

"What happened?" Delainey asked. It was like picking at a scab. She knew perfectly well that at any moment she'd go too deep and the wound would tear open and start to bleed. But she couldn't stop herself.

"Nothing big, really. It just was obvious that we were much better as friends than we ever would have been as husband and wife. And there was Jack."

There was something in Liz's voice… "What about Jack?" Delainey asked warily.

"That's the big news I was going to tell you over dinner.

He'll be on his way home in a few days, as soon as this cruise is over. He'd have come sooner but he was afraid the shipping line would sue him if he didn't finish out the three-month contract. Totally overresponsible. Thanks, Delainey. If it hadn't been for you…"

I'm just glad something I did worked out right, Delainey thought as she closed the door behind Liz.

She phoned the real estate office, and while she was waiting for the receptionist to put her call through to Patty she carefully arranged Sam's change on the breakfast bar. A circle of small coins formed the outline of a face, with a couple of quarters for the eyes, the knife forming an angry red slash of a mouth, and the diamond ring in the exact center to be the nose.

The receptionist came back on the line. "Hasn't she answered? I'm sorry, she must have left the building. Can I take a message?"

Delainey was just giving her number when she heard the click of a key in the front door. She put the phone down and swept her fingertips through the assortment on the breakfast bar until it was no longer recognizable as a face.

Sam stopped on the threshold, his hand still on the doorknob. Then, as if he was forcing himself to relax, he closed the door and set the calfskin briefcase on the floor.

Just act offhand, Delainey ordered herself. *If he can be casual, so can you.*

"I'm sorry I didn't see you drive up," she said. "It must have been quite a sight—the suit, the briefcase, and the motorcycle." Despite her resolution, pain welled up inside her, and suddenly she couldn't pretend anymore. "You could have told me, Sam. You knew I was no fan of Curtis Whittington's."

"No, that was clear," he agreed. "But there wasn't much you wouldn't do for the bank. Even when your job was on the line, you kept swaying back and forth, not believing it could come to that. One minute you were going to sell the town house, the next you weren't. You'd talk about looking for another job—but in the next breath you'd say that maybe if you waited a little longer you wouldn't have to. Every time I thought I knew which side you were going to land on, you changed your mind.''

She could see why it had looked that way. And to an extent, it was true—she had wavered like a willow in the breeze. It just hadn't been for the reasons he thought it was, and she wasn't about to explain what had really been going on.

''If you had warned Jason—''

Delainey was furious. ''As if I was interested in saving his hide!''

''Not for Jason's sake, no. But you would have tried to protect the bank.''

How could she deny it, when she'd been doing precisely that this afternoon?

''If you told him what I was doing, and he told Curtis, that would have been the end. Every shady deal, every questionable transaction, would have been smoothed out and covered up—for a while. Don't you see, Delainey? As long as I didn't know for sure where your loyalties lay, I couldn't take the chance. But you couldn't ruin things if you didn't know.''

''Oh, that makes me feel *much* better.'' Acid dripped from her voice.

''It should. You were an important part of this, you know. It took us both to break it open—you to get at the records and interpret what all the money-shifting meant, and me to put the pieces together from the corporate end.''

''I had it all wrong. I didn't think of money laundering till after you'd gone.''

''But finding those holding companies was the key.''

''Don't patronize me, Sam. One thing I don't understand,'' she said suddenly. ''Why didn't Curtis recognize you at the mansion that night?''

"I'd never met him before. There were four of us partners—that's why the company was called Foursquare in the first place. I was on the production end of things, and I almost never set foot in the office, so it was the partners on the business end who dealt with Curtis. By the time I started asking questions, they'd already been seduced by the offer and I was outvoted. But I doubt Curtis would remember my partners, either. We were just names on paper as far as he was concerned. That's why I figured it was safe to take a closer look at him that night and listen in on what he had to say."

And I sure helped out there. I'd like you to meet my fiancé.... "What's going to happen to Foursquare now?"

"Good question. Because the deal to purchase it was fraudulent, we might actually get it back—if there's anything left to get. But that's not why I wanted to stop Curtis."

"You've been working on it all this time?"

"Trying to. Curtis didn't make it easy. The terms when he bought the business not only included that clause which kept me from touching anything to do with electronics or electrical engineering for six months, but the new management put a gag order on the employees. If a Foursquare worker even spoke to one of the former owners, he was fired. So nobody was talking."

"No wonder you were suspicious."

"It seemed unnecessarily dictatorial—unless there was something to hide. Plus there was the fact that Curtis paid too much for the business. Foursquare was a nice little company, but it wasn't worth what Whittington paid for it. He explained that he was willing to give a premium price for the niche market we represented. But then when you told me that Foursquare wasn't paying its bills on time and they weren't dealing with George Laurent anymore—"

"I didn't tell you that," Delainey protested.

"Not in one chunk, and not in so many words, but you told me."

She remembered thinking that Sam had the memory of a tape recorder—but she hadn't realized that he was latching onto bits of information and fitting them together.

"I couldn't figure out why they suddenly didn't care anymore whether the parts they shipped arrived damaged."

"It was because electronic parts weren't the real product anymore," Delainey mused. "Money was."

"Exactly. Anyway, when I caught up with George and found out what was going on—"

Light dawned. "*That's* why you knocked those files off the credenza in Josie's office. Not to see what was in them, but so George wouldn't see you. Or rather, so I wouldn't see you and George having a reunion."

He nodded. "The last thing I expected was to run into George in your office—and I didn't want to explain right then how I happened to know him. I owe Josie a lot more than a box of chocolates for making that mess. Would she like to take her husband on a trip to the Caribbean, do you think?"

"Don't ask me. What are you going to do now?"

"For a while, it appears, I'll be spending my days with the district attorney and the white-collar-crime people. By the time that's over, my noncompete clause will have expired."

"And you can go back to work."

"You thought I didn't want to, didn't you?"

"I must have sounded pretty silly," Delainey said softly, "trying to line you up in the handyman business. Or to persuade you to go back to school… Hey, you told me you never finished. But if you're an electrical engineer—"

"With a perfectly good master's degree. I was just a few hours short of my doctorate when my buddies and I started Foursquare, and Gran hasn't forgiven me yet. Maybe I'll do that this winter—I can probably fit it in along with tinkering on this new idea.''

"New idea? I thought you said you weren't allowed to touch anything electronic.''

"I haven't been building it, just thinking about it. You can't stop a man from thinking. George has already figured out how to package it, so now I just need to make it work. He likes you, by the way.''

"I know,'' Delainey said dryly. "That's what got me fired. Maybe he'll make it up by giving me a job.''

Was it her imagination, or did Sam tense up? Having her working for his good buddy might not be his idea of heaven, she supposed.

But he sounded perfectly relaxed. "I heard your boss offer you the moon to stay.''

She nodded. "Unfortunately for him, it would take a few stars thrown in on top to make me do it.''

"The board asked Jason for his resignation right after you left the conference room. Or did you know that already?''

She'd thought that she'd slipped out so quietly that no one could have noticed. Had Sam been watching her? *Don't even dream about it.*

"I missed that bit of news.'' She considered it, and shook her head. "It doesn't really make much difference. RJ fired me without even hearing me out. It would be awfully hard to work for him after that.'' She sighed. "So after all the fuss, I'm right back in the same spot I was the day Jason took over. Only this time I'm doing something about it— I've listed the house for sale, and I'll be job-hunting after all.''

"Maybe you should have a chat with Gran.''

"What are you talking about?'' Emma was just about the last person Delainey would have thought of as an employment counselor.

"She thinks your idea of a business incubator for women is inspired."

"I know—I heard her telling Jason at the party. But it takes more than just a good idea to get something like that off the ground. My friend who's in real estate has a building in mind, and I've got a list of people who would jump at the chance to have offices there, but it's the financing I need."

"Talk to Gran," he said.

"About money? Sam, the woman's living with friends while she's waiting for her apartment to be ready. I'm not asking Emma to risk her retirement savings on a business incubator."

"I thought you believed in this idea."

"I do. But every investment carries the possibility of failure. I wouldn't take a chance with Emma's nest egg."

"Emma's nest egg," Sam said, his tone very precise, "was laid by the golden goose. She owns a good chunk of an insurance company, part of a property development firm, a heavy-construction outfit, and I don't know what all else. She can afford to take a flyer, and she thinks it would be a much more amusing pastime than insurance and heavy construction are."

Emma was wealthy enough to consider funding a business incubator as a *hobby?* "Sam, does she have any idea what kind of money I'm talking about here?"

"She thinks you could get a pretty good start with eight million." He leaned across the breakfast bar, put a fingertip under Delainey's chin, and raised her jaw back into place.

"Eight—" She swallowed hard. "It wouldn't bother you? If I was working with Emma?"

"Why should it bother me?"

Because I want it to bother you. I want you to be miserable that I'm working with your grandmother, but I'm not even seeing you. She shrugged. "No reason, I guess."

''That's it, then. Give her a call—Liz knows where she's staying. I'll pack up my stuff and get out of your way.''

She watched him cross the room and go up the stairs, and felt as if her heart was tying itself in a knot. In a few minutes he would be gone, and it would seem as if he'd never been a part of her life. The game was over, the farce was done.

And she shouldn't care. He'd used her, taken advantage of her...

She stared at the heart over the fireplace, and a voice echoed in the back of her mind. *He started it,* Liz had said.

And then she heard herself answering. *It doesn't matter who started it. What counts is that somebody is big enough to swallow their pride and stop it before it's too late.*

Of course, if she swallowed her pride—if she told Sam how she felt—the odds were pretty good that the only thing she'd end up with would be the world's worst case of indigestion.

But if she didn't, she would have to live forever with the heartache of knowing that she hadn't done everything she possibly could, because she was too scared to take the risk.

She didn't make a conscious decision, and before she realized what she was doing she was at the top of the stairs.

The door of the back bedroom was open, and Sam's suitcase lay atop a stack of boxes. It was empty.

He'd obviously heard her footsteps, for he turned away from the closet as she came in.

''Sam, I have to tell you...'' She stopped, not quite sure what she wanted—what she needed—to say. ''All that wavering back and forth I was doing...sell the house, don't sell it, look for a job, don't look. It wasn't the job and the town house I was anxious to hold on to.'' Her voice felt raspy. ''It was you.''

She saw the instant when he realized what she meant, and relief flooded over her.

Then his eyes grew hard. ''Because you thought I was

the kind of guy who was looking for a bed and three meals a day, and if you couldn't provide them I wouldn't hang around.''

This is going all wrong. ''No. I...''

''You thought if you brought home the bacon, I'd believe I was doing you a favor by eating it.''

''It would have been a sort of trade. People do it all the time. One works, one stays home—''

''It's different if it's a partnership. But you didn't expect that much from me, did you? What a great guy you think I am.'' Suddenly the rough edge vanished from his voice. ''Is there nothing you want for yourself, Delainey?''

The sudden gentleness gave her strength. ''Yes. There is.'' She closed her eyes and tried not to think about what she was saying, because if she paused to consider, she knew she'd never say it at all. ''Sam, will you make love to me? Just this once. No strings.''

The silence in the room was so heavy that she felt she couldn't breathe. Finally, she couldn't stand it any longer. She had to know. She opened her eyes.

He was watching her, waiting. ''No,'' he said. His voice was almost gentle.

She nodded, just a little. ''I'm sorry. It was...foolish of me.''

''Damn right it was foolish. That's not the kind of trade I'm interested in. I'm not going to live off you and make payments in bed.''

''Sam...'' she said uncertainly.

''You listed the house for sale, you said? Fine. Give me the name of the real estate company, because I'm buying it. I will not be your rent-free guest. You will talk to Gran, and the two of you will decide whether to start up the business incubator. If you decide not to do that, then you may look for a job if you wish. Otherwise you'll damn well—''

Her head was spinning. "Sam…you've made your point. I'm sorry."

He looked down at her, eyes narrowed. "No, I don't think I've made my point yet. *This* is the kind of trade I want."

He was across the room to her and she was in his arms before she could react.

He'd kissed her before in tenderness, in empathy, in comfort, and she'd wanted to melt into him and stay forever close. But this time there was nothing tender or empathetic or comforting about the way he held her. There was nothing gentle about his kiss. He was fierce, fiery, demanding—and in a wholly different but even more terrifying way, she wanted to cling to him so tightly that no one could ever tear her away.

She gasped, and instantly he let her go and she could breathe again. It was just that she didn't want to, if that was the price she had to pay for not being in his arms.

"Delainey." His voice was rough. "I'm sorry. I didn't mean— Oh, dammit, that's not how I meant to do this. I was going to leave you alone for a while, give you a chance to cool off and think…and then I was going to come back and tell you… Only I got up here and I couldn't make myself put anything in the suitcase."

"What were you going to tell me?" It was barely a whisper.

"That I hated keeping it all secret from you. At first, it didn't matter so much. But after a while—it was important, what you thought of me."

"I got that impression," she said wryly.

"No," he said as if he hadn't heard her. "That's not quite true. It was important from the very beginning. I just wasn't smart enough to know it yet. Even that first night when you tried to set yourself on fire—"

"I did not try to set myself on fire, Sam."

"—And I saw you standing by the fireplace in your satin

pajamas, I should have known. And then there was that night at the Mansion. You hit that nail squarely on the head, you know—you were doing just fine with Curtis and company. I was the one who was uncomfortable, because I was feeling possessive. When you announced that we were engaged, I felt as if I'd been kicked. It just took a while to realize that I reacted that way because it was what I wanted.''

She couldn't even move; it was so much more than she had hoped for.

"Delainey, I know it's too fast. I just— I'm crazy, I suppose.''

She laid a finger across his lips to quiet him. "Then we're both crazy. The day we decided to pretend we were engaged, and I told you it was you I had to have—I didn't know how true it was. I love you, Sam. I think I always have. That's why I claimed you that night. It was incredibly foolish, it was a stupid thing to do—'' She took a deep breath. "But it just felt right.''

His arms tightened slowly around her. "I think it was the smartest move you ever made.''

He kissed her long and hard, and then he laid his cheek against her hair. "There's one more thing we need to talk about, Delaney. Your ring.''

She tried to keep her voice light. "You mean Liz's ring, don't you? It's over on the breakfast bar.''

"She told you? I'll—''

"Not exactly. I figured out it was real, and I asked her who…'' *What happened before I knew him doesn't matter. It's none of my business.* But she couldn't stop herself from blurting out the question anyway. "Why did you keep it, Sam?''

He held her a little away from him. "Have you ever tried to sell something like that?''

He sounded quizzical, which was the last reaction she'd expected. "Well—no. Of course not.''

"Let me tell you, it's next to impossible. The jeweler wouldn't take it back, and people who want to buy a diamond ring through the classified ads prefer one that actually looks like a diamond."

Delainey bit her lip to keep from smiling. "Liz's taste is…unique."

"You can say that again. After a couple of tries, I gave up and decided that whenever Liz and Jack have a baby, I'll turn the damned thing into a christening bracelet. Anyway, that's not the ring I was talking about."

Delainey frowned. "There's *another* one? How many times have you been engaged, Sam?"

"Only once that matters." He reached into his pocket. "I said we needed to talk about *your* ring, Delainey. This one, if you like it."

He held up a ring—a slim gold band almost bare of decoration, except for an enormous, pear-shaped, pure white solitaire diamond.

Delainey started to cry.

Sam looked worried. "It was silly, I suppose, not to let you choose—but it made me feel better to have it in my pocket. If you don't like it…"

She dashed away the tears. "I'd hate to put you to the trouble of trying to sell another one… Oh, Sam, are you nuts? It's the most beautiful thing I've ever seen!" She held up her left hand, fingers outstretched.

He slid the ring onto her finger, and it nestled down as comfortably as if she'd always worn it. It was even precisely the right size.

Delainey mopped away the last tear. "Anything else we need to get straight?"

"If you find me lying around the house," he said, "it'll be because I'm working out an electronics problem in my head, not because I'm lazy."

"Okay," Delainey said meekly. "Are you going to be? Lying around the house, I mean?"

"This house? Our house?"

She nodded.

"Count on it. And one more thing. I won't make love to you just this once, with no strings attached. I intend to make love to you frequently, and there are going to be lots of strings attached—including a marriage license. If that doesn't suit you, too bad—because that's how it's going to be."

"It suits me," she managed to say, as he kissed her. And then there was no more need for words.

HARLEQUIN®
INTRIGUE®

Our unique brand of high-caliber romantic suspense just cannot be contained. And to meet our readers' demands, Harlequin Intrigue is expanding its publishing lineup to include **SIX** breathtaking titles every month!

Here's what we have in store for you:

❏ A trilogy of **Heartskeep** stories by Dani Sinclair

❏ More great **Bachelors at Large** books featuring sexy, single cops

❏ Plus outstanding contributions from your favorite Harlequin Intrigue authors, such as Amanda Stevens, B.J. Daniels and Gayle Wilson

MORE variety.
MORE pulse-pounding excitement.
MORE of your favorite authors and series.
Every month.

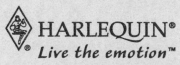

HARLEQUIN®
Live the emotion™

Visit us at www.tryIntrigue.com

HI4TO6B

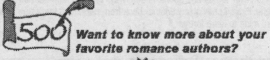

If you enjoyed what you just read,
then we've got an offer you can't resist!

Take 2 bestselling love stories FREE!

Plus get a FREE surprise gift!

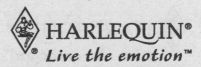

Harlequin Romance®

A wedding dilemma:

What should a sexy, successful bachelor do if he's too busy making millions to find a wife? Or if he finds the perfect woman, and just has to strike a bridal bargain...

The perfect proposal:

The solution? For better, for worse, these grooms in a hurry have decided to sign, seal and deliver the ultimate marriage contract...to buy a bride!

Will these paper marriages blossom into wedded bliss?

Look out for our next Contract Brides story in Harlequin Romance®:

Bride of Convenience by Susan Fox—#3788

On sale March 2004

Available wherever Harlequin books are sold.

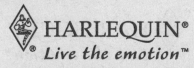